MW00941043

The Last Of The Navel Navigators

David Hailwood

Book 1 in the Navel Navigators series

Biomekazoik Press

This First Edition published in Great Britain in 2018 by
Biomekazoik Press

Copyright © David Hailwood 2018

www.davidhailwood.com

The right of David Hailwood to be identified as author of this work
has been asserted by him in accordance with the Copyright, Designs
and Patents act 1988

This book is a work of fiction and any resemblance to actual persons,
living or dead, is purely coincidental.

All rights reserved. No part of this publication may be reproduced,
stored in a retrieval system, or transmitted in any means, electronic,
mechanical, photocopying, recording or otherwise, without the prior
permission of the copyright owner, except in the case of brief
quotations with proper reference, embodied in critical articles and
reviews.

Cover design by Brett Burbridge

Biomekazoik Press logo by John Kirkham

ISBN: 1986050483
ISBN-13: 978-1986050487

With thanks to Jenny Hailwood for her extensive knowledge of shoes, Brett Burbridge for his artistic genius, and Dave Swann for the goat lore.

1

Deliverance

It was Erasimus T. Rigwiddle's last assignment. He was sixty years old today. Fifty-five of those years had been spent working as a courier for the Swift Wings Delivery Service, and the five years before that had been spent training to become a courier for the Swift Wings Delivery Service. As a stork, career options were extremely limited; it was either deliver babies for a living, or join the unemployment line.

So it was just as well that Erasimus loved his job. In his long, distinguished career he'd delivered babies to all five corners of planet Hotchpotch, for all manner of races. He'd delivered Sprites, Fairies, Goblins, Elves, Humans, Demi-humans, Semi-humans, Dwarves, Navigators, Orks, Sporks, Spiggots, Gollythrashers…one time he even managed to deliver a Troll. The lads back at the depot had said it couldn't be done, but by crikey he'd shown them what for!

Of course, that had been back in his younger days, before he'd become afflicted with bad hearing, a dicky heart and twenty million miles on the clock. Nowadays, even the tiny sleeping bundle secured in the delivery satchel strapped across his waist caused him to wheeze and splutter every flap of the way.

Time to retire gracefully, whilst there was still life left in this old sky-bird.

Tomorrow he would hang up his wings for good, buy a little place in the countryside and settle down with a nice lady stork. Then, if he was extremely lucky, perhaps another stork would bring them a child. A dragon, maybe. Interspecies adoption was all the rage these days – orks were adopting fairies, dwarves adopting ogres – so he didn't see why he couldn't adopt a dragon. After all, who wanted a plain old boring ordinary baby when you could have one that was multi-coloured, fireproof and heated the house at night?

Yes, a Red Fanged Raxithorian Bird Hunting Dragon. That was the one for him! He'd have to teach it to stop hunting birds, of course. But that was all part of the joys of fatherhood. One final challenge to see him through his twilight years; was that really too much to ask?

Crrkkk! '–asimus!' a tinny voice barked in his left ear. 'This is Control! Are you reading me, over?'

'Reading you loud and clear, Control!' Erasimus piped back into his headset. 'Nothing but clear blue skies and plain sailing up ahead. Looks like I'm in for a frightfully dull end to an otherwise rip-roaring, seat of the britches, thrill packed career,' he sighed.

Crrrkt! 'Don't count your chickens whilst there's a fox on the prowl, Erasimus,' the air traffic controller crackled back. 'We have a severe weather warning! There's the mother of all storms converging on your position. And it looks like it's brought its family!'

Erasimus' eyes scanned the horizon. There was barely a cloud in the sky. 'Are you sure about that Control?'

'Absolutely certain,' the voice said sharply. 'Be advised: it's coming in fast, over.'

The light dimmed, the sky blackened and the heavens began to rumble…

'Ah, now this is more like it!' Erasimus grinned, as the rain lashed down upon him and the wind tossed him violently from side to side. 'Dashed decent of you to lay on a monsoon for me, Control. Please be sure to convey my heartiest gratitude to the Weather Wizards. They've really excelled themselves this time.'

Crrrkt! '–othing to do with the Weather Wizards, Raz. It came out of nowhere. 'Fraid I'm going to have to order you to set down immediately and return to the depot on foot.'

'What?' Erasimus shrieked. 'Abort the mission and walk home with my bally tail feathers between my legs? Never! I'm a flyer, and proud!'

The rain was coming in thick and fast now, making Erasimus' flight goggles steam up. He could barely see the beak in front of his eyes, let alone the ground that lay a thousand feet beneath his wings. 'Not once in my entire career have I failed to make a delivery,' he said, urging himself onwards, 'and I'm certainly not going to start now. Not on my last da –'

A fork of lightning stabbed down through the sky and struck him across the tail feathers.

The smell of cooked chicken filled the air.

His beak coughed and spluttered, his wings seized up.

Suddenly he was falling.

'Mayday! Mayday!' Erasimus cried. 'I'm going down!' A thick plume of smoke trailed out behind him. 'Cargo has been lost! Repeat, cargo has been lost!'

Below him, the delivery satchel tumbled end over end, its singed and tattered strap flailing helplessly in the wind. From inside there came a noise, growing louder and louder and louder.

It was the sound of a baby crying.

'I'm coming, lad!' Erasimus hollered. He pointed his beak downwards, and launched into a dive. 'Just you stay put now.'

His only hope was to reach the satchel before it hit the ground. Then perhaps at the moment before impact he could cushion it with his own frail body.

'By Jove, what a dashingly heroic way to punch one's ticket,' Erasimus enthused. 'The gods must be smiling on me today!'

G-force rippled his feathers. His scarf whipped around like a crazed King Cobra.

Just when he was so close he could almost touch the satchel with the tip of his wing, something wholly unexpected happened.

The satchel began to glow bright blue.

'Oh!' Erasimus said, barely able to keep the sense of wonder out of his voice. 'You're one of those sort of babies are you?'

With a brilliant explosion of light and a deafening '*Whuuuuuuuuuuuuuumph!*' the satchel simply winked out of existence. Where it had been mere moments before, there was nothing left but a fading trail of stars.

In the deep dank wilderness of Southern America's Sasquatch County, two foul-smelling dungaree-clad yahoos stood staring at a scorched delivery satchel that dangled precariously over the swamp, its strap tangled in a tree branch.

It had appeared out of thin air moments ago, and had given rise to much speculation.

'What d'you think's in it Pa?' the youngest of the two – a scraggly, buck-toothed teenager named Shawney – said, scratching his buttocks. 'Munnee?'

'Nah. Gators wouldn't be that interested in money,' the eldest – a stocky balding brute called Kleetus – responded, motioning to the beady reptilian eyes that watched patiently from under the murky waters. 'They got nuffin' to spend it on, see?'

Shawney's mouth split into a grin so wide that it exposed all seven of his yellowed teeth. 'They could use it to buy shoes, Pa!' he yelled. 'Gator shoes. To replace the ones them poachers keep stealin'.'

Kleetus rolled his eyes at the heavens. 'Shawney,' he growled, 'don't make me fetch yer Ma now, y'hear?'

Shawney glanced warily at the hefty stick leant up against a tree next to Kleetus. It was seven feet long, thick as a tree trunk and had the word 'Ma' etched lovingly into its side. 'I'll be quiet, Pa,' he whispered.

'Atta boy, Shawney.'

As something began to move around inside, the satchel started to bob up and down on the branch. Kleetus and Shawney watched with renewed interest.

The branch creaked ominously.

'It's gonna fall, Pa,' Shawney said.

'Yup.'

'We prob'ly oughta do somethin'.'

'Yup.'

'We could always throw rocks at it,' Shawney suggested.

'Nope.' Kleetus picked up his stick and strode towards the edge of the bank. 'Got me a better idea.' He leant out as far as he could, stretched out an arm and hooked the strap with the end of the stick. Carefully he drew the satchel back across the water. The gators snapped at it as it passed by overhead, as if to say 'oi!' and 'that's my lunch!'

When it was safely within Kleetus' grasp he placed the satchel down on the ground, plunged in his thick, hairy arms and rummaged around inside. His fingers closed around something warm and soft.

'What is it, Pa?' Shawney asked, attempting to catch a glimpse over his father's broad shoulders. 'Food? Riches?'

'No Shawney, it's a…it's a…' Kleetus slowly drew his hands out of the satchel. Cradled within them was a newborn baby boy. He had been wrapped in a bright yellow blanket that had 'express delivery' stamped upon it in red. 'It's a buh…a buh…a buh –' Kleetus stammered, as the baby stared up at him through big, curious eyes.

'A big pink jellybean!' Shawney cried.

'Not quite, son,' Kleetus said, regaining his composure. 'What we have here is a real live genuine baby.'

Shawney leant in closer and inspected the child. He let out a guffaw. 'No wonder his parents didn't want him,' he snorted. 'He's only got ten fingers, and none of his toes are webbed!'

'Poor little tyke,' Kleetus said, as the baby attempted to suck at Shawney's eleventh finger, and spat it back out, realising something wasn't right. 'Looks hungry.'

'We got some cheeseburgers back at the ranch,' Shawney said.

Kleetus' eyes widened as the alarm bells of unexpected fatherhood sounded in his mind. 'Now hold on there, Shawney!' he said sternly. 'We can't possibly keep 'im. Bringin' up a child takes a lot of responsibility. He's not like them chickens I brought yer last Christmas. Fer one thing, the chances of eggs is unlikely.'

'But no one else wants him, Pa,' Shawney whined. ''Xcept the gators, and I don't reckon they've got his best innerests at heart.'

Kleetus cast his eyes around the swamp. There was no one else around for miles; Ma's reputation had made sure of that. 'You got a point there, son,' Kleetus said, eyeing the child thoughtfully. It gurgled at him, and blew a snot bubble. For Kleetus that was the deal clincher. 'I guess it would be useful to have a spare pair o' hands around the house, fer doin' chores and the like.'

'Them dishes still need doing, Pa,' Shawney said brightly.

'I don't think he's quite ready fer the dishes yet, Shawney,' Kleetus said, gently placing the baby back in the satchel and fastening it up. 'We'll start him on the smaller jobs first. Gator wrestlin' and that.' He grabbed the satchel by the strap and hoisted it over his shoulder.

'What we gonna call him, Pa?' Shawney asked, as they stomped their way through the undergrowth, heading back towards their weather-beaten shack.

'Don't rush me, Shawney,' Kleetus said. 'I only just got round ta namin' you.'

2

A Beastly Birthday

Thirteen years passed.

Kleetus finally thought of something.

'Jellybean!' he cried, pointing a finger at the scrawny dark-haired youth who was dragging a mop around the kitchen floor's impenetrable layers of grease, cheerfully spreading it from one place to another. 'From now on, yer name's Jellybean.'

The youth paused momentarily in his duties and gave his father a sidelong glance. 'Why's that then, Pa?' he asked.

Kleetus' thick brow caved in as he tried to remember what had sparked the idea in the first place. 'Don't ask awkward questions, boy!' he snapped. 'Do you want yer present or not?'

'Yes please, Pa,' Jellybean said. 'It's a great name. Just what I've always wanted!' Since Jellybean's previous names over the years had ranged from 'Boy', 'You There' and 'Not Shawney' to 'Snot Nose', 'Stink Face' and 'Gator Bait' it was certainly the best he could hope for.

A wide grin spread from ear to ear. He'd only been awake ten minutes and already he'd been given a new mop and a new name. This was going to be the greatest birthday ever!

'If you think that's good, jest wait 'til yer see yer next present.'

Jellybean's eyes gleamed. 'There's more?'

Kleetus stepped to one side and gestured grandly to the pile of dirty dishes that sat festering in the sink. 'Today,' he declared, 'you become a man!'

'I'm not sure I like the sound of that, Pa,' Jellybean said. The light in his eyes faded as he looked upon a mountain of crockery that towered high into the sky, poking out through one of the many holes in the roof. From a distance it appeared as if the shack had two chimneys, except one of them was covered in flies rather than soot.

'Be grateful!' Kleetus growled. 'Most boys your age only get nasty old cake fer their birthdays. What you're gettin' is a lot more valuable. And you know what that is now, don'tcha?'

'Responsibility,' Jellybean intoned.

'That's right. Responsibility!'

'I'd prefer cake.'

Kleetus tossed him a rag that was almost twice as dirty as the dishes. 'Once yer done there, go make a start on the gator pit.'

'But Pa –'

'No buts!' Kleetus snapped. 'I want them gators clean enough to eat my dinner off. Same goes fer them dishes, or you an' yer Ma'll be havin' very stern words.' He stomped out, swishing his stick through the air as he went.

'Yes, Pa,' Jellybean sighed.

He held the dishcloth out before him for protection and took a tentative step towards the washing up, like a priest with a crucifix advancing on a nest of vampires.

This was going to be the worst birthday ever.

Grrrruuumbbble rumble rumble rrruuuumbbbbllle!

Jellybean lay in the barn in his tatty Gator Bait pyjamas (the ones with a picture of a cartoon alligator on the front, biting a man's legs off), hands clutched over his ears, desperately trying to ignore his digestive system's cries for attention.

By the time he'd gotten a small portion of the dishes clean enough to eat off of, there'd been nothing left for him to eat; he'd missed breakfast, lunch and supper. There was always the possibility of a midnight snack, but once he'd bypassed the tripwires, snake pits and bear traps that Kleetus left to defend the pantry, it would probably be breakfast time again.

Rruuuummmmble rummmbbblle rumbbble!

The only one to answer his stomach's distress signal was Brian the goat, and that was clearly something he did with reluctance. He ambled over from his corner of the barn, his ears twitching away in annoyance, and dropped a half-eaten boot down beside Jellybean's bed.

'Um, I'm all right for boots thank you Brian,' Jellybean said.

Brian looked expectantly from Jellybean to the boot, and then pushed the boot closer.

'It's not that I don't appreciate the offer, but I'm really not that hungry.'

Grrrrumbbble rrrrumble squiiiiiiirkk!

Brian eyed Jellybean's stomach suspiciously.

Jellybean was quick to realise that if he didn't get his rumbling under control soon he might well be eating that boot whether he liked it or not. He cast his eyes around the barn, hoping to find something to take his mind off food. Other than hay bales and cow dung, there was precious little in the way of entertainment.

He looked up. The stars were out, twinkling away through the cracks in the rafters. They were his friends; he knew them all by name. Not just their constellation names, such as Cassiopeia, Orion, Ursa Major and Aquarius, but by their individual names. He decided to recite them.

'Sparkly Trevor, Shiny Mildred, Kluktruut The Unkind, Nondescript Norman, Skrofrekruktulthrax The Unpronounceable, Nimtec The Misbegotten –'

A cloud drifted across the night sky, blocking his view. Usually Jellybean could see the stars with crystal clarity, even in the daylight, but hunger was breaking his concentration.

As the enormous pressure of another gargantuan rumble welled up inside him, his eyes strayed down towards his stomach.

There, nestled in his bellybutton, was the answer to all his problems.

Fluff!

An unnaturally large build-up of fluff.

There was enough there to keep him occupied for a good few hours, if he paced himself. He decided to pick at it a while, hoping the sheer monotony of the action would be enough to send him to sleep.

Pick   pick   pick   pick   pick   pick   **click!**
WHUUUUUUUUMMMMMFFFFF!

The barn was bathed in a brilliant blue light and a glimmering portal opened from out of nowhere. At its centre a vortex of stars shimmered and swirled, almost as if someone had pulled the plug out of God's bathtub, and the entire universe was going down the drain.

Jellybean froze, unable to tear his eyes away. Something inside the portal was winding its way towards him.

A mysterious robed figure stepped out, framed by the light. His features were obscured by an enormous pair of metallic glasses that whirred and clicked like an angry insect as its lenses adjusted to focus on Jellybean. In his hand he held a small cylindrical device that emitted a constant beep.

'*Target identified!*' announced the device suddenly. '*Commence dialogue!*'

'Eh?' said the figure. 'Oh, right. Yes, the speech!' He thrust the device into his robe's top pocket and marched purposefully in Jellybean's direction. 'Do not be afraid!' he bellowed. 'I am Caspian Thrall! Revered Techno Mage from the city of Chromebrood, and I –' Something went 'squish' beneath his feet. He looked down and grimaced. '…have just trodden in a cowpat,' he sighed. 'Terrific.' He sat down on a hay bale and scrubbed at the sole of his boot. 'Bear with me a moment, oh mighty one,' he said, waving a handful of soiled straw in Jellybean's direction. 'Technical difficulties.'

Jellybean watched with detached interest, relieved that he seemed to have finally fallen asleep.

As dreams went, this wasn't a particularly good one. Usually there were monsters, or at the very least an explosion or two. Tonight his imagination was clearly as starved as his stomach.

'Halfway across the universe for this,' the mage muttered. 'Absolutely typical.' He got to his feet and cautiously weaved his way towards the foot of Jellybean's bed, making doubly sure to avoid any cow related obstacles. 'Right,' he said, looking from Jellybean to Brian. 'Which one of you lads is the Navigator?'

Jellybean stared at him blankly.

'Me-e-eh?' said Brian.

'Ah! Fantastic!' The Techno Mage bowed down grandly at Brian's feet. 'At last, my liege! You have summoned me!' he declared. 'I am so happy that I, Caspian Thrall, am the one you have chosen to protect you on this quest! Long have I prepared for this moment. My heart is a glowing beacon of pride. My body is strong, my spirit is willing, my shoe smells vaguely of cowpat, but let us not dwell on such matters! Command me, my liege! Command me!'

He paused a moment, waiting for an answer.

'Bleeeh,' said Brian, poking out his tongue.

The mage slowly raised his head and looked into Brian's eyes. 'Well what sort of a command is that?' he sneered. 'If that's the best you have to offer we're not going to get very far on this quest are we?'

'Um,' Jellybean said.

The mage thrust out a hand for silence. 'Don't interrupt. I'm talking to the all powerful Navigator here.'

'No,' Jellybean said, in the slow measured voice he usually reserved for explaining simple tasks to Shawney. 'That's a goat.'

The mage squinted at Brian. He removed his glasses and rubbed his eyes. Without them his face instantly lost its air of mystery and Jellybean was surprised to discover he was a lot younger than he'd expected. Judging by the feeble cluster of hairs on his chin, and the ridiculous pencil moustache that looked like it was badly in need of an eraser, the mage had only recently thrown off the shackles of puberty to make an undignified break for adulthood.

'You're right,' Caspian said, upon completing his inspection of Brian's stocky four-legged form, 'it is a goat. Sorry about the mix-up – got a bit blinded by the light there.' He put his glasses back on, got to his feet, cleared his throat, and bowed down grandly before Jellybean. 'At last, my liege, you have summoned me –' he began.

Before he could get any further, a hideous decaying stench filled the air; an overwhelming reek of such repugnancy that Jellybean was grateful for the first time today that he hadn't actually eaten anything. The Techno Mage was not so fortunate. He coughed and gagged, and buried his head in his robe. 'All right, own up,' he said. 'Was that you or the goat?'

It was neither.

More shapes were forming inside the portal; inhuman things that writhed and slithered. They arrived in the portal's opening as one huge pulsating mass of claws and teeth, struggling with each other to break through and claim their prize. Their eyes, of which some of them had many, were all focused on Jellybean.

'By the Great Wizard's gizzards!' Caspian exclaimed. 'You didn't close the portal!' He cast off his robe, revealing an impressive suit of armour covered in tiny shimmering circuits, and jabbed a button on the palm of his glove. A crackling white staff of pure energy materialised in his hand. 'Back!' he yelled, leaping between Jellybean and the portal to bar the way. 'Go back to the foul chasms that spawned ye!'

The creatures snarled and snapped their defiance.

'Go on!' Caspian cried, giving his staff a mighty shake. '*Push off!* Don't make me tell you twice!'

A slimy green tentacle lashed out and knocked him to the ground.

Jellybean squealed with delight as it slithered towards him. Now this was more like it! This was the sort of dream he usually had, filled with weird bug-eyed creatures and endless life-threatening situations. Finally his imagination had perked up a bit.

'Close the portal!' Caspian commanded.

Jellybean's delight turned to horror as he felt the cold, wet touch of the tentacle on his foot. It felt hideously real. 'H-h-how?' he stammered.

'What do you mean "how"?' Caspian cried, rolling to avoid a swipe from a pair of claws almost twice the size of his head. 'Put your finger back in your bellybutton! It's not that difficult is it?'

The tentacle began to coil its way around Jellybean's body, pinning his legs, working upwards towards his arms. Hurriedly he thrust a finger in his bellybutton.

Click!

The portal flickered briefly, but remained. The tentacle's grip tightened.

'Well?' Caspian yelled as he struck a nameless horror in the unmentionables. 'What are you waiting for? Give it a poke!'

'I have!' Jellybean wheezed.

'Then why is it still here?'

Jellybean didn't reply. He was too busy having the life slowly squeezed out of him.

'Something must be mimicking the portal's frequency,' Caspian said. He scanned the writhing mass of creatures, cycling through the settings on his glasses; he tried Infra Red, Ectoplasmic Green, Thermal Imaging, Ethereal Imaging, Optical Illusion, Dark Aura, Light Aura, and Twilight Resonance. Finally, he removed the glasses and used his eyes. They instantly fell upon a repulsive rotting hag with lank grey hair and a gigantic elongated jaw that hung down to her waist. She stood in the centre of the portal, swaying from side to side, pale eyes turned to the heavens as she expelled a ghostly melody from the depths of her haunted soul.

'Aha! A Screaming Heebie-Jeebie!' Caspian enthused. 'These are very rare. You should feel privileged.'

'Gluk!' said Jellybean, struggling to remove the tentacle wrapped around his throat.

'There's only one way to deal with a creature like this,' Caspian announced. 'And since I don't know what it is, I guess I'll have to find another.' His eyes darted around the barn until they settled on

Brian, who'd retired to a corner to eat his boot in peace. 'Hey, you! The hairy fellow! Bring that over here.'

With a snort of indignation, Brian ambled over and spat the boot out at Caspian's feet.

'Much appreciated.' Caspian picked up the boot by its laces, swung it round his head a few times to gather momentum, and let go. With a sickening crunch it struck the old hag square between the eyes, breaking her concentration along with her nose.

There came a blinding flash of light as the portal winked out of existence, taking the snarling slithering beasts with it.

'That takes care of that,' Caspian said, powering down his energy staff and donning his robe. 'Good thing there wasn't more of them. Get three Heebie-Jeebies in a room together and they start singing folk music. Very rare to survive that ordeal.' He patted Brian, who was staring forlornly at the spot where the portal had been, clearly wondering where his boot had got to.

Jellybean shook himself free from the twitching severed tentacle, and dived beneath the bed covers. Caspian strode over and pulled them back down. 'Okay kid,' he said. 'What have we learnt today?'

'Bu-bu-buh –' stammered Jellybean, his face almost as white as the sheets he was hiding in.

'That's right,' Caspian said. 'Keeping a portal to the Other Worlds open for longer than necessary is extremely bad. Make a mental note of that. It could save your life.'

'Wh-wh-wh –'

'What were those things?' Caspian finished for him. 'Dark creatures, from dark dimensions. They want your power for themselves to use for, ooh, dark purposes I should imagine. Seems to be their style.'

'W-w-what power? I don't understand.'

'There's a time and a place for everything, my liege.' Caspian leant across and laid a comforting hand on Jellybean's shoulder. 'All you need to know is now that I'm at your side, standing loyal and firm, no harm will ever come to you.'

A food tray at the far end of the barn clattered to the ground. Shawney stood in the doorway, staring wide-eyed at the strange man stooped over his younger brother's bed.

Caspian stared back at him. 'Yes?' he said eventually. 'Can I help you?'

'*Paaaaaaaa!*' Shawney yelled. 'There's a man in a dress in the barn wiv Jellybean!'

'It's a robe, actually,' Caspian muttered.

Kleetus' gruff voice called back from the out-house. 'Is it Cousin Henry?'

Shawney looked Caspian up and down. 'No Pa,' he hollered. 'It ain't Cousin Henry.'

The outhouse toilet flushed with urgency. 'Go fetch me Petunia!'

A wicked grin stretched across Shawney's face. 'Yer fore it now!' He fled the barn, heading for the shack.

Caspian picked up an apple that had rolled towards him, and shined it casually on his robe. 'Who's Petunia?' he asked. 'His wife?'

The wall of the barn beside him exploded, showering him in splinters.

'No,' Jellybean replied. 'His shotgun.'

Another hole exploded in the wall. Shawney's ugly face peered through it. 'Yer missed again, Pa,' he said.

Caspian dived headfirst into a haystack and attempted to bury himself. 'Open a portal!' he cried. 'Open one now!'

'B-b-but what about the beasts?'

'I've got news for you, pal – the beasts are already at the door, and they're armed! Now get us out of here!'

FOOOOOOOOOOOM! went Petunia, carving yet another jagged hole in the wall.

At this rate there wasn't going to be much left of Jellybean's bedroom. He reluctantly poked a finger in his bellybutton and opened another portal.

Caspian made a mad dash for it, scattering hay in every direction. 'Come on! Excitement and adventure awaits! Follow meeeeeeeeeee!' He leapt into the portal and vanished, buckshot flying overhead.

Jellybean stared into the shimmering blue haze. It had been quite an unusual day really, and he was starting to consider that closing the portal, curling up in bed and pretending none of this had ever happened might be the best thing for all concerned. Let that strange man in the dress have all the excitement and adventure he could handle; in the morning, Jellybean still had dishes to do.

Just as Jellybean was about to give his bellybutton another poke, Brian's ears pricked up, and with an excited bleat he ran full pelt towards the portal's opening.

'Brian! Wait!' Jellybean cried. 'I'll get you a new boot.'

But it was too late. The goat had already vanished.

That settled it. Jellybean swung his legs over the edge of the bed, put on his snuffling pig slippers and headed towards the portal.

'Jellybean!' Kleetus yelled, poking his furious face through a hole in the wall. 'Get back here and finish your chores!'

'I'm just going to fetch Brian,' Jellybean said, giving his father a reassuring wave from the mouth of the portal. 'I'll be back in a minute.' He took a deep breath, closed his eyes and stepped forwards into the unknown.

3

Small World

Apart from experiencing a slight chill, and his ears going 'pop', little else happened to Jellybean on his journey through the portal. In a fraction of a second, it was over. When he opened his eyes, he was stood on the dull grey surface of an alien planet. He scanned the surroundings, expecting to at once be bombarded by breathtaking unearthly sights that would thrill him to his core.

Well, there was none of that.

All this planet had was a tree. It was an extremely tall tree, granted, but it wasn't worth travelling fifty billion light-years for. On closer inspection Jellybean noticed shoes of every shape and size dangled from its branches, almost like someone with no imagination had put them there in a desperate attempt to 'alien' the place up a bit.

The only one to appreciate the effort was Brian. He lay on his belly beneath the tree with a satisfied smile, gorging on a first class banquet of high quality footwear.

Above him, Caspian sat on a branch, staring out across the dismally short length of the planet's surface. He was convinced that if he looked hard enough he would probably catch sight of the back of his own head.

'Door!' he hollered.

Jellybean waggled a finger in his ear. 'Eh?'

Caspian gestured towards the portal illuminating Jellybean from behind. 'Unless you want demons to pull off your face and wear it as a hairnet, my liege, I'd advise you close the door.'

'Oh.' Jellybean jabbed a finger in his bellybutton. The portal vanished.

'Interesting choice of destination for our first adventure,' Caspian said, his voice tinged with doubt. 'Seems to be a little bit lacking in excitement and perilous situations, if you want my professional opinion. Still, at least we won't be left wanting for shoes, eh?'

'I'm just here for my goat.' Jellybean scratched Brian affectionately behind the ears. 'Come on, boy.'

Brian let out a disapproving bleat, slightly muffled by a size twelve loafer.

'Yes, you're quite right.' Caspian leapt nimbly down from the tree, his robe flaring out around him. 'I think we've already exhausted this planet's potential. Let's forge ahead to pastures new. Might I recommend as a stop-off point the fabled golden planet of Teltamarok? Imagine that! An entire planet made of solid gold! Or perhaps the sun-kissed virginal shores of Roserrica. Rumour has it the women there wear naught to cover their modesty but really, really large hats.' A leer spread across Caspian's roguish features. 'We could do a lot of good deeds on a planet such as that. A lot of good deeds!'

'I think I'm just going to go home, actually,' Jellybean said, the idea of a planet full of scantily clad women holding little appeal for him. After all, the only woman he'd ever known in his life was his Ma, and she was a stick.

'Oh, I see,' Caspian smirked, his feeble moustache twitching away in amusement. 'Too young for women, too grubby for riches eh?'

'Grubby?' Jellybean attempted to smooth down the creases in his pyjama top. A button pinged off, shortly followed by another, leaving one solitary button holding the defensive line.

'Don't fret, I have the perfect remedy for that sort of thing.' Caspian delved a hand into his robe and rummaged around. He drew out a handful of sweets in brightly coloured wrappers. 'Tailors' Toffees!' he declared, thrusting them under Jellybean's nose. 'Best in the land. All you need do is suck away, and a snug-fitting outfit will instantly form around you.'

Jellybean reached out a tentative hand, and then stopped as one of the rare pieces of advice his father had given him took root in his mind. 'Don't take sweets from strangers, boy!' Kleetus had warned one hooch-addled evening. 'Or they'll steal yer pigs! It happened to Cousin Henry and it could happen to you. Worst part is them strangers didn't even give Henry no sweets. They jest took 'is pigs! Take heed, young Gator Bait. Take heed and be warned, yessir!'

'They come in a whole variety of fashions and flavours,' Caspian continued, oblivious to the red flush of hillbilly rage spreading across Jellybean's face. 'There's the traditional Navigator's outfit, or if you fancy something a bit more flamboyant perhaps you'd care to try Urban Pirate or Aquatic Ninja?'

'Get yore thieving hands off my pigs!' Jellybean hollered suddenly, bunching his hands into fists.

Caspian's thin lips stammered open and shut, as his brain tried to process this somewhat extreme reaction to toffees. Slowly, he put the sweets away. 'There, the nasty old sweets have gone. Your goat-pig's safe.'

'Come on, Brian. We're leaving!' Jellybean poked a finger into his bellybutton and opened up a portal. Brian trotted towards him with a quintet of shoes clutched in his teeth by the laces.

'That's just charming that is!' Caspian roared. 'You're going to leave me here? Just like that?' He threw his head back and swooned theatrically. 'Whilst there's adventuring to be done? Damsels to be rescued? Villains to be smited?'

'Yes,' Jellybean said. 'I don't actually know you.'

'Of course you do! Everyone knows the great Caspian Thrall.' He thrust out his chest, and flashed a well-practised grin. 'Where I'm from, children sing songs about my exploits!'

'Well they don't where I'm from,' Jellybean replied. 'Where I'm from, children sing songs about other children bein' ate by gators.' He took a step towards the portal.

'Fine!' Caspian hurriedly changed tactics. 'Far be it for me to stand in the path of a child's destiny, even if said destiny happens to be something as trivial as beddy-byes time.' He turned his back on

Jellybean and marched haughtily off into the bleak grey nothingness of the planet. 'I guess I'll just have to teach all these *fabulous magic tricks* of mine to someone else,' he called loudly as he walked. 'I was going to take you under my wing, show you the works, tricks of the trade, but no. I guess it simply wasn't meant to be. I guess I was wrong about you. I guess –' Caspian broke off suddenly when he realised he'd marched full circle around the planet, and was back where he'd started. He turned around. The portal had vanished.

Brian and Jellybean remained.

'You know magic?' Jellybean breathed.

Ever since Shawney had shown him the 'got your nose' trick at a young age, he'd been desperate to learn more about the mystic arts. Even though it had turned out to be someone else's nose that Shawney had found in the swamp earlier that day, it had still left a lasting impression.

'Do I know magic?' Caspian leant against the tree and beamed. 'Do the triple-buttocked Wingnut people of the Metakula Plains wear Raboolian Hiking Trousers?'

Jellybean blinked in confusion. 'I don't know,' he said. 'Do they?'

The Techno Mage shrugged. 'Not sure. Never met them myself. Now, let's do some magic!' He rolled up his sleeves and wiggled his fingers in a mysterious fashion. 'Think of number. Any number. It can be any number at all. Six. Three. Nine. Twelve. Anything.'

'Seven,' said Jellybean.

The mage frowned. 'Don't tell me the number. It's not going to be much of a trick if you tell me the number, is it?'

'Oh. Sorry.' Jellybean's eyes drifted away from the mage, and settled on the tree. It was an incredibly tall tree. He began to wonder what might be at the top.

Caspian waved his hands at the sides of Jellybean's head. 'I'm in your mind…' he declared. 'I'm prowling around…I'm crossing the garden path of your subconscious…' He paced around the tree with his eyes closed, taking mighty strides.

Jellybean grabbed hold of a low-hanging branch, and pulled himself up. If his Pa's bedtime stories about Lumber Jack the logger's son were to be believed, he'd find a giant's kingdom at the top, where he'd be able to acquire the priceless egg of a golden moose.

'I'm at the gate to your brain…' Caspian hollered from the ground. 'I've unbolted its door…I'm sneaking inside…'

Up Jellybean climbed, past loafers, brogues, sandals, clogs, wedges, pixie boots, stilettos, flip flops, pumps, slip-ons, mules and court shoes.

A solitary pair of faded blue trainers caught his eye, and he sidled across the branch towards them. Although discoloured and sticky, like overripe fruit, he plucked them and slipped them on.

Perfect fit! He let his slippers fall to the ground and continued upwards, marvelling at the comfort of his new footwear.

'Sneaking…sneaking…' Caspian's voice was a whisper, carried on the wind.

The higher Jellybean went, the smaller the shoes around him got, until eventually they were little more than well-polished buds sprouting from dangerously thin branches.

Just as he began to consider going back down, a shrill rasping from above caught his attention. He dug his thin fingertips into the bark, and continued onwards. As he climbed, he became aware of hundreds of tiny little notches carved into the tree trunk, like someone had been patiently counting the days as they passed.

Pushing upwards through a canopy of green wellies, he discovered the culprit; a weathered old stork, clad in a scarf, hat and leather flight goggles. It was perched on the topmost branch, a thin trickle of drool dangling from the end of its beak as it snored noisily away.

The poor creature looked like it had been half-plucked, then cast aside in favour of a healthier meal. Jellybean had seen more promising specimens in Shawney's taxidermy collection, and most of them were missing their heads.

One thing was certain; it didn't look the sort of bird to lay a golden egg.

With a sigh, Jellybean began his descent.

Caspian was still taking purposeful strides around the trunk. 'The number's there! I'm approaching it from behind…sneaking… sneaking…'

Jellybean dropped the last few metres to the ground, and watched as the mage covertly scrawled something on his palm.

'Aha! Got you, you little rascal!' Caspian launched his hand into the air and snatched at an invisible number. His eyes flickered open, and he thrust his palm forward until it was inches away from Jellybean's startled face. 'Is *this* your number?' he cried boldly.

There was a number seven written on it.

'No,' Jellybean said.

The mage's triumphant grin faded. 'What? You said it was a moment ago.'

'I changed it.' Jellybean looked around for his goat. Brian was buried beneath a pile of footwear, attempting to eat his way out.

'You can't just change it! The trick doesn't work if you keep changing it.'

'I only changed it the once.' Jellybean took his goat gently by the horns, and pulled him free.

'I've written seven now,' Caspian whined. 'That's indelible ink, that is. It won't come off easy.'

Jellybean shrugged. 'Sorry.'

The young mage stared thoughtfully at his hand. 'I suppose I could always turn it into an eight. Your numbers not eight, is it?'

'No.'

'How about seventeen?' The pen was out again and hovering over his palm. 'I could do a seventeen.'

'No.'

Caspian smiled hopefully. 'Seventy one?'

'You're not a very good magician are you?' Jellybean concluded.

He opened up a portal and led Brian through.

4

Bagoolah-Bagoon

Stars flashed briefly before Jellybean's eyes. He stepped out the portal, and plummeted.

Wind whistled through the numerous holes in his pyjamas as he attempted to work out why he was descending through the neon yellow sky of an alien planet at such an alarming rate.

When he looked up, the reason became clear; the portal had opened several thousand feet above the planet's surface. It shimmered and winked above him, like it was sharing a private joke with the universe. He couldn't reach it. There was no way back. The landscape was a distant speck, growing larger by the second.

'Meeeh!' said Brian, as he tumbled through the air.

'Sorry, Brian! I thought this was home.'

Caspian fell past, shuffling a deck of cards. 'All right, pick a card. Any card.' Wind whipped them from his hands, scattering fifty-two aces. 'Hey, where'd the ground go?'

Jellybean pointed a trembling finger below.

'Well what's it doing down there?' Caspian's puzzled frown gave way to a crafty smile. 'Oh, I see! This is a test isn't it, my liege? You want to see another demonstration of my wizardly worth.'

'I'm good, thanks,' Jellybean said. His words were drowned out by the roaring wind.

'Right, let's see what life-saving devices I've got in my pockets.' Caspian thrust a hand into the folds of his robe, and pulled out a miniature trumpet. His eyes widened. 'But first,' he said, attempting to conceal his surprise, 'perhaps a little mood music?'

Jellybean squeezed his eyes shut, and searched for the Navigator buried deep inside. After following the guiding light of a star across vast metaphorical mountains, deserts and oceans, he found him, sinking in the swamp of his subconscious.

His eyes snapped open, sparkling like a clear night's sky. 'Maybe I could try closing the portal above us, and opening one below us?' he suggested.

Caspian blew a victory note on the trumpet. 'Excellent plan, my liege.'

Jellybean stuck a finger in his bellybutton and twisted.

As the portal above closed, something raced through – a creature, moving at incredible speed, its wings a blur.

It was heading straight for him.

'Demon!' Jellybean cried. The sparkle faded in an instant.

'Terrific,' Caspian said, as he disappeared through a thin layer of clouds. 'I love a challenge!'

The creature's ragged wings beat vigorously as it closed the gap between itself and its prey. Its talons spread, and it let out a victorious cry.

'Chocks away! Pip pip! Tally-ho!'

Gnarled claws clamped around Jellybean's shoulders with a gentleness that surprised him. He looked up, expecting to glimpse the scaly red under-side of a demon in flight. Instead there were hundreds of tatty grey feathers, attached to the withered body of a large stork.

'Erasimus T. Rigwiddle, at your service.' The stork snapped off a quick salute with the tip of a wing, and spiralled into a dive.

Wind tugged at Jellybean's pyjama bottoms with renewed vigour.

'Come on, wings! Keep up!' Erasimus wheezed. 'Just a…small…child…' His beak rose. Wings straightened. 'You've…carried…a troll.' Gradually, he drew level. 'Ah, that's better. Sorry about that. Bit out of practice.' The stork stretched out its scrawny neck, and squinted at Jellybean through the brown leather flight goggles perched on top of its beak. 'Item number 7769857. My, how you've grown!'

'Most people call me Jellybean,' said Jellybean. 'Or Stink-face, but I prefer Jellybean.'

'Well, dear fellow, as an expert courier for the Swift Wings Delivery Service, it's my sworn duty to deliver you to your rightful owner, or die trying!' The stork puffed out his fragile chest with pride.

A distant funeral dirge played on the trumpet, to the accompaniment of mournful bleating.

Jellybean glanced down at the tiny figures tumbling towards the landscape. 'What about my friends?'

'Sorry. Not part of the order.'

'But they'll die!'

'Nothing wrong with a heroic death,' Erasimus enthused. 'Would've had one myself, if I hadn't got caught in your portal's backwash and marooned in a shoetree for thirteen years.'

'I'd rather live, if it's all the same to you,' Caspian's voice yelled as the ground drew closer.

'In that case,' Erasimus hollered back, 'you might want to look out for that –'

A mountain struck Caspian with astonishing force, and catapulted him into the air. He sailed upwards past Jellybean, Erasimus, and Brian, without so much as a scratch on him.

'Meeeeh!' said Brian, as he crashed into the ground, and bounced into the air.

'Evasive manoeuvres! Incoming goat! Mayday! Mayday!' Erasimus banked left as Brian whizzed past.

Caspian dropped down screaming, and then flew upwards doing a pirouette.

'What's going on?' Jellybean asked, watching his two companions bounce up and down on the planet's surface, giggling and bleating like maniacs.

'Isn't it obvious?' Erasimus asked. 'This must be Bagoolah-Bagoon!'

'I beg your pardon?'

'A giant inflatable planet.'

As the stork drifted closer to the landscape, Jellybean noticed the hills and mountains had a distinctly plastic shine. Closer inspection revealed a flock of inflatable sheep scattering across the hills, as they were pursued by a vicious pack of inflatable wolves.

'Safest place in the solar system,' Erasimus said. 'Though its inhabitants live by a rather strange mantra. What was it now? Ah, yes: "No somersaults, no shoes."'

'Brian!' Jellybean hollered. 'No shoes, mate.'

'Meeeh!' grumbled Brian, as he let the last remaining shoe slip from his mouth. It bounced up past him, and he gave chase.

'If this place is inhabited, where is everyone?' Jellybean scanned his surroundings, eager to see a real live inflatable alien.

'It's not so much inhabited as occasionally in use. The Navigators use it as a training ground for their young.' The stork's aged eyes flitted between the deserted landscape below, and the equally sparse sky above. 'Come to think of it, the place should be teeming. Most unusual!'

Brian flipped past, pulling a face. Jellybean squirmed around in Erasimus' tight grip.

Erasimus sighed. 'You want me to let go, don't you lad?'

Jellybean smiled sheepishly. 'If you wouldn't mind.'

Erasimus released his grip on Jellybean's shoulders. 'Go have your five minutes of fun then. And take those bally shoes off!'

'Wheeeeeeeeeeeeeeeeeeeeeeeeeeeeeeeee!' yelled Jellybean as he plummeted towards the planet's surface.

Erasimus tucked in his wings and dived after him. 'As the saying goes: "When in Bagoolah-Bagoon, do as the Bagoolahs' do!"' He rocketed down past Jellybean, twisted nimbly round Brian, loop-de-looped past Caspian, and thumped face-first into the side of a hill.

Where he stuck, like a dart.

Erasimus awkwardly withdrew his beak, accompanied by the unsettling *'hssssss!'* of air escaping. 'Ah yes, I remember the rest of that sacred mantra now,' he said, as the landscape started to deflate around him. '"No somersaults, no shoes, no sharp objects." That's how it went.'

Caspian thumped into the ground, and this time failed to bounce. Instead, he started to sink. 'Nice going, birdbrain! You've punctured the planet!'

Mountains drooped and hills folded in on themselves.

'Perhaps now would be a jolly marvellous time to return to Hotchpotch?' Erasimus said as Jellybean and Brian thudded down beside him. 'If you'd be so good as to plot a course.'

Jellybean attempted to get to his feet. It was like trying to stand on top of a plate of jelly, during an earthquake. 'Plot a what?'

'A course, dear boy! Plot a course.'

Jellybean stared blankly at the stork. An inflatable cow flew past, mooing in alarm as it was sucked up into the sky.

'The planet's starting to lose its atmosphere!' Caspian screeched. 'If you don't act fast we're going to start falling upwards.'

'Come on, lad,' Erasimus encouraged. 'Use that star chart in your head. Mind map our way to victory!'

'Eh?' Jellybean's frown deepened.

'Look, it's just a simple matter of correlating the stars position with the data on the navigation chart stored in your brain, calculating the distance, velocity and party weight ratio, and we're homeward bound.'

Jellybean's lips moved silently, as he tried to work out what 'correlating' meant.

The ground wobbled dangerously beneath them.

'Just poke a finger in your bellybutton and get us the hell out of here!' Caspian yelled.

'Oh, right.' Jellybean followed Caspian's directions to the letter. A portal whummed open. Caspian leapt through, propelled by one final bounce. Jellybean went for a somersault, Brian a triple flip.

'Now hold on a moment!' Erasimus cried. 'You can't just –'

He was already talking to thin air.

5

Giant Freezer

Jellybean brushed himself down and looked around at his new surroundings. Solid ground beneath him, blue skies above, and nothing but rolling hills and countryside stretched out in every direction.

'Booooring!' Caspian said, stifling a yawn. 'Off to the next planet.'

After waiting a moment for Brian and Erasimus to emerge, Jellybean closed the portal and opened up a new one.

'Stop, stop, stop!' Erasimus snapped. 'What in Hotchpotch's name do you think you're doing?'

'Navigating,' Jellybean said, closing the portal again.

'That's not navigating! That's just poking a finger in your bellybutton and hoping for the best.'

'There's a difference?' Jellybean and Caspian said together.

Erasimus clacked his beak in annoyance. 'Of course there's a difference! If you don't take time to plot a course first we could end up anywhere in the entire universe.'

'Isn't that rather the point?' Caspian said. 'We're on an adventure. Last one to kill a goblin horde's a rotten egg. Wehey!' He powered up his staff and swished it through the air, beheading a patch of particularly menacing-looking daffodils.

'Aside from the fact that some of my best friends are goblins,' Erasimus said, scowling at Caspian, 'I'd rather not adventure straight into the middle of a black hole. If we're to arrive on Hotchpotch in one piece, I must insist that proper safety precautions are exercised.'

'You're the one who just popped a planet,' Caspian mumbled under his breath.

'That's beside the point. Now, start plotting that course!'

'How?' Jellybean asked.

'It's perfectly simple.' Erasimus unfurled a wing towards the sky. 'Look to the stars and find the one that resembles Hotchpotch.'

'Oh brilliant, we'll be here for hours.' Caspian slumped down on a tree stump and crossed his arms. 'In case you haven't noticed, it's daytime. If we're going to have to wait for the stars whenever we leave, we're not going to get f–'

'That one,' Jellybean said, pointing without a moment's hesitation towards a star no one else could see.

Caspian switched his glasses to their highest magnification and squinted up at the sky. 'Which one? It's just clouds.'

'Good show, dear boy,' Erasimus said. 'Take us to that one then.'

Fixing his eyes on the distant star, Jellybean opened a portal. An icy wind rushed through from the planet that lay beyond, sending a shiver down his spine and up his pyjama legs.

'Feels more like planet of the Chilly Willy's to me,' Caspian muttered, drawing his robe around himself for warmth. 'You sure the kid's going to be all right in just his jammies?'

'He'll be fine,' Erasimus assured him. 'The Weather Wizards maintain a nice even temperature over the planet. At this time of the year we should be in for sunny spells with the occasional light shower.'

They stepped through into a raging blizzard.

Fierce winds whipped at them from all sides. Jellybean clung to Brian, afraid of being swept away across the desolate white landscape, never to be seen again.

'Guess those Weather Wizards must be on strike, eh?' Caspian switched his glasses to 'defrost' mode and searched for the nearest available cover. His eyes settled on a cluster of snow-encrusted mounds, and he made towards them.

Jellybean trudged along behind, sinking deeper into the snow. 'Do you want me to c-c-close the portal?'

'No point,' Caspian yelled, pitching his voice above the howling wind. 'I doubt we'll be staying long.'

'I've never known it to be so cold!' Erasimus puffed out his feathers. 'Something terrible must've happened.'

'P-p-perhaps it's that global freezing my Pa's always on about,' Jellybean suggested. '"Sling more tyres on the bonfire, lad!" he always used to s-s-say. "Do your bit for the planet now!"'

Caspian stopped suddenly, and squinted at the unusual mounds they were approaching. 'Is it my imagination,' he said, 'or does that hill have a face?'

The rest of the party stopped and stared.

'And kneecaps!' Erasimus yelled, looking further down. 'I definitely see kneecaps.'

'Toes!' Jellybean cried, pointing excitedly at the far end. 'I can see toes.'

There were indeed toes: enormous blue ones, which poked through the snow's crust like bizarrely formed icicles.

'Me-e-e-e-eh!' said Brian, attempting to draw attention to the most unusual sight of all – a colossal frost-covered arm that reached upwards out of a mound, clutching in its frozen fingers a large red plastic spade, like the sort a child might use on a daytrip to the beach.

Jellybean stood transfixed by this unusual spectacle. The creature was at least fifty metres long from head to toe. His nose was as big as a ski-slope, ears large enough to park half a dozen Range Rovers inside, mouth drawn into a wide grin, exposing teeth the size of boulders and some truly atrocious dentistry. 'A giant!' he breathed.

Caspian shrugged. 'I've slain bigger.' The lens on his glasses extended, and his finger strayed towards a button as he lined up a photo.

Jellybean began to picture the creature when it was alive, taking mighty strides across the landscape, crushing buildings beneath its feet, scooping up livestock and devouring them whole whilst villagers scattered like ants.

Erasimus scowled at the giant, as if mystified by its existence.

Caspian snapped a quick photo of him. 'Someone you knew?'

'Of course not!' Erasimus said irritably. 'Hotchpotch doesn't have giants. Us storks couldn't deliver them. Would've broken all sorts of health and safety regulations.'

'Then what's it doing here?'

'The answer is simple, dear boy,' Erasimus sighed. 'We're on the wrong bally planet.'

'Raaaaaaaaaaaaaaarrrrgh!' yelled Jellybean as he stomped past, waving his arms around wildly, in pursuit of Brian.

'Another fine piece of navigating, my liege,' Caspian commented. 'Let's head back before we become a frozen mystery for the next hapless bunch of explorers.' He span on his heel and marched off towards the portal, struggling against the wind like a deranged mime artist.

Erasimus hopped from one foot to the other. 'You don't seem to appreciate the gravity of the situation! Our young Navigator doesn't have a clue what he's doing. Without proper knowledge of his powers, we'll be left navigating blindly around the universe.'

'So we take the scenic route,' Caspian called back over his shoulder. 'So what? Now come on, get a move on! We've only got twenty seconds.'

'Twenty seconds?' Erasimus beat his wings frantically in an attempt to catch up. 'Twenty seconds until what?'

'Until portal demons rush through and tear us all to shreds.'

Erasimus squawked in amusement. 'Portal demons? Preposterous! There's no such th–' With the speed of a striking rattlesnake, a massive purple tongue lashed out from inside the portal, coiled around Erasimus and drew him back into its depths, leaving a scattered trail of feathers swirling in the air.

'Meeeh!' said Brian in alarm.

'By the Great Wizard's gizzards!' Caspian screamed. 'A Collywobble!' He reached for the button on his glove, but the creature was too quick for him.

The tongue lashed out again, once, twice, three times.

Before Jellybean could react, he found himself being thrust headfirst into the enormous slavering jaws of a portal demon.

6

Porridge Slides And Beard Pixies

Down they went, sliding deeper and deeper into the Collywobble's gullet, propelled by an enormous wave of saliva.

Just when they thought things couldn't get any worse, the oesophagus ended, disgorging them into a pool of thick grey sludge in the pit of the demon's stomach.

They thrashed and kicked to the surface and lay floating amongst the congealing lumps.

Sludge ran down Caspian's face, clogging his ears, filling his nose with its pungent aroma. 'What is this stuff? Do I even want to know?'

Jellybean licked his lips. 'Tastes like porridge.'

'Meeeh!' agreed Brian, as he doggy-paddled past with his mouth open.

'Don't eat it!' Erasimus snapped. 'It's hardly likely to be sanitary.'

'Hmm,' Caspian mused, having a bit of a taste himself. 'Needs sugar. And perhaps a blob of mustard.'

'Mustard?' Erasimus' eyes flared. 'Are you insane? You can't put mustard on porridge! Mashed earwigs or nothing, that's what I say.'

'I had roaches in mine,' Jellybean said grimly. 'Didn't mean to. They just sort of fell in.'

They slumped out onto the undulating mass of veiny pink flesh that lined the creature's stomach.

'Good God!' Erasimus shuddered in disgust. 'I may never eat blancmange again!'

Squirmy bits, wriggly bits and purple knobbly things lay scattered all over the place, like the left-overs at a butcher's banquet.

'Come on Brian, out you get,' Jellybean said. 'You're going to give yourself indigestion.'

'Meeeeh!' said Brian. He paddled towards them, and heaved himself out.

Caspian scraped the lumps out of his hair, and scooped several massive dollops out of his pockets. 'Oh, well, that's just perfect, that is! I'm going to get complaints about this, you mark my words.'

'Complaints?' Erasimus tore his eyes from their grizzly surroundings. 'From who?'

'The other Techno Mages who share my pockets.' Caspian sat on a wobbling mound, unbuckled a boot, and tipped out some goop.

'You let other people use your pockets? What-ever for?'

'I've got Deep Pockets,' Caspian said, as if this somehow explained everything. He unbuckled and emptied the other boot.

'Right.' Erasimus squinted at Caspian's earlobe, clearly wondering whether his brain was full of por-ridge. 'Good for you.'

'Oh no, bad. Very bad.' Caspian shook his head solemnly. 'If the other mages complain, the department head might change the pocket's frequency. Then where would I be?'

'Your pocket has a frequency as well, does it? My my!'

'And a wormhole,' Caspian enthused. 'Just a small one, mind.'

'Well, yes.' Erasimus nodded, perhaps a little too vigorously. 'It would have to be.'

'Anyway, let's not stand around here talking about my amazing Deep Pockets.' Caspian clapped his hands together. 'Let's go take a look around this beauty.'

'You can't be serious!' Erasimus squawked. 'This is hardly the sort of place for a spot of sight seeing.'

'Just think,' Caspian said as he squelched off across the uneven landscape, 'we could be the first people in the entire universe to see the inside of one of these magnificent beasts.'

'I wouldn't be so sure about that,' Jellybean said, as they rounded the side of a large pink quivering mound, and were greeted by the sight of a ticket booth with an overweight dwarf in it.

He was clad in a top hat and tailcoat, and sported a filthy-looking beard that rippled in a most peculiar fashion. His fcct were resting on the counter as he thumbed lazily through a copy of 'Hi-Ho' magazine.

'Tickets?' he asked, without looking up.

'I beg your pardon?' said Erasimus.

'You wanna go inside, you have to buy a ticket.'

'Go inside? What are you blathering about, man? We're already inside. We just got swallowed by a demon!'

'Nah, mate,' the dwarf said, 'I mean inside the carnival.'

'There's a carnival?' Jellybean's eyes lit up.

The dwarf chuckled. 'Wouldn't be much of an attraction if there was just one dwarf and a coupla beard pixies, would it?'

'Bearded pixies?' Erasimus scoffed. 'No such thing.'

'Not bearded pixies,' the dwarf said, giving them a withering look. 'Beard pixies. Pixies that live in beards. It's perfectly simple.'

'I've never heard anything so ridiculous in all my life,' Erasimus said. 'And I've had a particularly long and ridiculous life.'

'All right then, cop a load of this.' The dwarf put the magazine down on the counter and bellowed: 'Turrrrn!' Suddenly his beard parted and three pixies wearing green leotards and funny little hats with bells abseiled down towards his magazine, using ropes woven from beard hair.

'Ayiyiyiyiyiyiyiyiyiyiyiyiyiyiyi!' they hollered. With an almighty heave, they turned over the page, and then scampered back up, whooping and cheering.

Erasimus stared wide-eyed and open beaked in amazement.

Even Brian temporarily stopped gnawing at a green wobbly thing he'd found.

The dwarf settled back in his seat, and smiled smugly. 'I'm a God to these people.'

Caspian slapped a porridge-stained wallet on the counter. 'How much do you want for them? Money is no object.'

'Oh I don't own the beard pixies, mate. They generally go where they please.'

'So why are they living on your face?' Caspian critically inspected the dwarf's ugly round features.

'Like I said, I'm their God.' The dwarf thrust a finger up a nostril and re-enacted the age-old dwarven tradition of mining for boogers. 'Wasn't intentional. They just happen to worship big beards. Now, are you gonna buy a ticket or what?'

'Actually, I think we'd best be heading on our way now,' intoned Erasimus.

'What?' cried Jellybean.

'You're kidding?' said Caspian.

'No skin off my beard,' said the dwarf. He plucked a grape from a bunch and threw it in the air. A tiny lasso lashed out from his beard, caught the grape mid-flight, and swung it expertly into his mouth.

Erasimus strolled out of earshot of the dwarf, and beckoned them over. 'There's something fishy about this whole set-up,' he hissed. 'Think about it. A carnival inside a demon's stomach, with porridge slides and beard pixies? Does that sound plausible?'

'Dunno,' Jellybean said, 'I've never been inside a demon before.'

'Yeah,' said Caspian. 'Maybe they've all got carnivals in them.'

'I think it's likely we're experiencing a mass hallucination brought on by the demon's stomach gas. The sooner we get out of here, the better.'

'Couldn't we just have a *little* look?' Jellybean pleaded.

'Best not to chance it; our brains could be turning to mush as we speak. Be a good chap and open up a portal.'

Jellybean looked to Caspian for assistance.

'It's your call, my liege,' said Caspian. 'You're the Navigator.'

'Any chance you could hurry things along, gents?' the dwarf hollered. 'It's just the beard pixies need to muck out the unicorns in a minute.'

'Unicorns?' said Jellybean.

'Hallucinatory unicorns,' Erasimus corrected. 'It's all in our minds. We're not really here. There isn't really a dwarf, and there most certainly aren't really beard pixies.'

Jellybean wasn't really listening. Ignoring Erasimus' squawks of protest, he rushed back to the ticket booth, with Brian and Caspian tagging along behind. 'Three tickets for the carnival please.'

'I shall defend you with my life on the dodgems, my liege,' said Caspian, dipping into his wallet. 'You do have dodgems, right?'

The dwarf shrugged. 'We've got rides that crash. Same principle, really.'

'Might as well make it four tickets,' Erasimus muttered. 'We're better off sticking together, in case one of us imagines something unspeakably unpleasant.'

Caspian thrust a handful of green notes covered in zeros and ones under the dwarf's nose, then shook them against his beard, trying to tempt the pixies. 'Keep the change, my good man.'

The dwarf frowned. 'What do I want with funny bits of paper?'

'That's three hundred binary widgets, that is. You could give yourself a full makeover. Mow the eyebrows, prune the beard, pluck those rampant nose hairs.'

'I don't care if it's ten million Jumbly Whoppers, mate,' the dwarf growled. 'It ain't legal tender.'

Jellybean's porridge-caked features sagged. 'So how are we supposed to get inside?'

'Use the wotsit. Universal Currency Converter.' The dwarf motioned with his eyebrows towards a large rectangular machine next to a turnstile at the entrance to the carnival.

Caspian strolled up to it, and gave it a critical appraisal. It had a small slot for coins, and a larger one for notes. 'Seems fairly straightforward.' He fed in a note and pressed a button. The machine clicked, whirred and clunked, then fell silent. 'Nothing happened!'

'So insert more shiny paper,' said the dwarf.

Caspian fed in another note, followed by another and another and another, until finally, once his wallet was completely empty, a single wooden token popped out. 'That's it?' Caspian said, turning the token over in his hands. 'That's all I get for three hundred binary widgets? One lousy token?'

'It may be binary widgets to you, mate, but to the machine it's just bits of paper. Everyone's got paper. Hardly a rare commodity, is it?'

'What's this part for?' Jellybean asked, pointing at a large hatch on the machine, marked 'other'.

'That's for other currencies, innit? You've got yer coins, you've got yer notes and you've got yer other.'

'What sort of other currencies?'

'It accepts pretty much anything really,' the dwarf shrugged. 'Everything's worth something, somewhere in the universe.'

'Except money, it seems,' Caspian muttered darkly. He handed over his token to the dwarf and exchanged it for a ticket.

A thought occurred to Jellybean. He thrust a hand into his pyjama pocket, and pulled out a brown apple core, and a ball of string. He fed the apple core to Brian, and the ball of string to the machine.

After a few clicks and some really meaty whirs, fifty wooden tokens shot out. 'Hurrah!' he cried, gathering them up in his hands and rushing to the ticket booth.

Caspian glared at Jellybean, then remembered his oath of allegiance and redirected it at the dwarf. 'How come he gets fifty tokens for a ball of string, and I only get one for my entire life's savings?'

'Very valuable, balls of string,' said the dwarf, nodding sagely. 'They comes in all sorts of use.'

Jellybean exchanged three tokens for tickets and crammed the rest into his pockets.

'That oughta leave you with more than enough to pay fer rides and refreshments. Doubt you'll be havin' much fun though.' The dwarf grinned at Caspian.

'On the contrary,' said Caspian, marching towards the currency machine. 'Watch and learn!' He rolled up his sleeves, plunged both hands deep into his pockets, and began to pull out a seemingly endless mass of unusual items, including: a French horn, three cans of Spam, a bunch of flowers, The

Fabled Screaming Skulls of Tiantantukka (gift set), twelve beer mats, a walnut, laser pistol, chest of drawers, the Norwegian flag, a set of adjustable spanners, pot noodle, senior citizen's bus pass, tax invoice, a pink ladies' bicycle, lawn mower, and an exciting range of hair care products.

'How the devil did you fit that lot in there?' Erasimus asked.

'I told you. Deep Pockets.' Caspian fed the items one by one into the hatch in the currency machine. A continuous stream of tokens flooded out.

Suddenly the machine beeped and a panel lit up, displaying the words 'insufficient tokens. Please consult vendor!'

'I don't believe it!' the dwarf cried. 'You've... you've emptied the machine!'

'And filled my pockets,' Caspian said, shovelling handfuls of tokens into his robe. 'Not literally, of course. They're far too deep for that.'

'No one's ever emptied the machine before.' The fat folds of the dwarf's face wobbled in distress. 'Now the pixies'll have to refill it. Backbreaking labour, that is. It'll take 'em hours.' He tapped impatiently at his beard. 'Come on, hop to it then.' The dwarf's beard was deathly silent. He parted it and rummaged within, turning up little else than chicken bones and the occasional piece of cheese. 'Where are you hiding, you little perishers?'

Caspian grinned. A trio of tiny tongues poked out of his beard, and blew raspberries at the dwarf.

'What? But...but how?' the dwarf stammered.

'Haven't you heard?' Caspian pushed through the turnstile, and strode grandly down the path, handfuls of tiny little rose petals scattering the route as he went. 'I'm a God to these people!'

7

Inner Demon

The carnival inside the demon was a mishmash of bright lights, gaudy colours, and overenthusiastic vendors all frantically trying to outdo each other in the excitement and entertainment stakes.

'Halfling Bowling!' bellowed a large ogre as they passed. 'Endless fun! Impossible to stop once you've begun!'

'Palms read!' cried an old crone. 'Fortunes told! Destinies unravelled! Prophecies fulfilled! Shoes mended!'

'Coconuts!' yelled another vendor. 'Coconuts! Come an get h'your things that look like coconuts!'

'Throw the ring on a unicorn's horn,' urged a yellow-skinned hobgoblin, 'and win yourself a pony ride!'

Jellybean and Caspian raced from tent to tent, spending tokens like there was no tomorrow. So many new sights, sounds and ways to be sick; it was almost too much.

Erasimus perched himself next to a food stall for the duration, tutting and shaking his head. Occasionally, thick globules of slime from the fleshy pink roof above dripped down and landed on him, which did little to improve his mood.

Whilst he was preening his feathers for the fifty-seventh time, Caspian dashed over and handed some tokens to the food vendor. 'Candyfloss and a toffee apple please.'

'We need a refill,' Jellybean explained to Erasimus, grinning from ear to ear. 'I threw up on the Wheezing Warlock.'

'Jolly good,' Erasimus said, though his expression suggested it wasn't. 'I see you even bought the t-shirt to prove it.'

'My pyjama top was getting a bit porridgy.' Jellybean looked around. 'Where's Brian?'

Caspian waggled an admonishing finger at Erasimus. 'You said you'd keep an eye on him.'

Erasimus gestured to a distant carousel, where a goat was going round and round, gradually turning greener. 'I did, but then I got dizzy.'

'As long as he's enjoying himself,' Jellybean said, 'that's the main thing.'

'Bleeeeeeh!' said Brian.

'There's yer candyfloss and toffee apple.' The ogre vendor handed over the items.

As Caspian brought the candyfloss to his lips, the pixies leapt out and stuck to it like flies in a web. 'Get out of it, you little rascals!' he snapped.

Erasimus grimaced. 'Disgusting horrid sticky stuff.'

'And there's your cone of mushy maggots.' The vendor handed a wriggling cone to Erasimus.

'Ah, now that's more like it.' Erasimus squeezed a generous dollop of ketchup onto the writhing mass, and dipped in his beak. 'Mmm! Been years since I've had mushy maggots,' he beamed. 'Just like my dear old mother used to regurgitate.'

Jellybean's face drained of colour. 'I think I've found a less fun way to be sick.'

'Let's go look in the House of Freaks,' Caspian said, gingerly plucking the pixies from his candy-floss and returning them to his beard. 'That'll put a smile back on your face.'

Jellybean tugged at Erasimus' wing. 'Come with us, Raz?'

'I hardly think the freak house is the sort of place for an upstanding member of the community.'

'I wouldn't be so sure,' Caspian said. 'They've got a birdman.'

'A fellow avian?' Erasimus' features softened. 'I must admit it would be nice to converse with one of my own kind.' He stroked his beak, deep in thought. 'Okay, but after this, I really must insist we leave.'

They entered a large tent that everyone else was giving a wide berth. When they emerged some time later, Erasimus was scowling harder than ever.

'Birdman, my beak!' he muttered. 'An over-sized conk and a liking for worms does not make a proper birdman.'

'I thought the Cyclops was pretty neat,' Jellybean said.

'He had two eyes!'

'Yeah, but one of them was slightly larger than the other. And he kept the small one closed most of the time.'

'How about that humpless hunchback?' Caspian said. 'Now there was a genuine marvel. You don't see one of them every day.'

'Yes you do. They're called "humans". Now come on, let's be having that portal. Chop chop!'

'Just one more ride on the Spitting Serpent,' Jellybean pleaded.

'We agreed that after the freak house that would be it. I've been patient so far.'

'But…but…'

'It's a big universe out there, full of exciting possibilities,' Erasimus reasoned. 'At some point in the journey, we're bound to get eaten by demons again.'

'Awww…okay,' Jellybean grumbled.

They retired to a quiet spot behind the harpy enclosure. Jellybean took one last look at the carnival, and reluctantly poked a finger in his bellybutton.

Click!

A few tiny blue sparks crackled in the air around him, then faded to nothing.

He tried again, with more vigour.

Click!

Not even a single spark.

Click click click click *clickety clickety* BANG!

Jellybean looked down. A thin wisp of smoke trailed from his bellybutton.

'Oh nice going,' Caspian said. 'You broke it!'

'I tried to warn you,' Erasimus said. 'But nobody listens to an ageing sky-bird, oh no…' He wafted the smoke away with a ragged wing. 'Now you've over exhausted yourself, it'll take a full eight hours' sleep to recharge.'

'You mean we're stuck here?' Caspian and Jellybean exchanged glances.

Erasimus nodded. 'A serious situation, as I'm sure you'll –'

'Hurrah!' they yelled, and rushed off to play on the Mermaid Rodeo.

Erasimus sighed wearily. 'I'll secure us lodgings for the night then, shall I?' He noticed a troll in orange coveralls dutifully shovelling harpy dung into a thick brown sack, and approached it. 'Excuse me my good…er…' Erasimus studied the troll's craggy features.

'Don't ask me, mate,' the troll thundered in a voice like an avalanche. 'I don't even know what gender I am.'

'Right, yes, well I was wondering if you could possibly direct me to a place of lodgings? Doesn't have to be anything grand. An unoccupied tent, or an uncrowded stable perhaps?'

'There's a hotel one stomach over,' the troll rumbled. 'Only four star, mind.'

'I say! How many stomachs does this beast have?'

'Ooh, lots,' said the troll. ''Ave you visited the one with the crazy golf course yet? It's an absolute blinder. Got a life-sized windmill on it and everything.'

'Perhaps later,' said Erasimus.

'Right-ho.' The troll went back to its shovelling. After a moment, it realised Erasimus was still staring. 'Something else I can do for you?'

'Assuming that this isn't just one big hallucination, I was rather curious to know how all you carnival folk got here.'

The troll heaved its massive shoulders. 'Used the porridge slide, didn't we? 'Course, in my days it weren't porridge they were usin'. It were swarms of bees. Not a popular choice, that one.'

Erasimus watched the crowds bustle through the carnival. 'You mean that the demon ate every single one of you?'

''S right. Crafty thing keeps popping up all over the place, thrusting his tongue through cracks in dimensions and 'oles in reality.' The troll paused a moment to lean on its pitchfork. 'Not sure why ee does it really. 'S not like ee does much digestin'.'

'A habitual overeater, eh?' Erasimus shook his head. 'Someone ought to employ a demon hunter to sort the bally rascal out.'

'Oh, they did.' The troll grinned amiably. 'Ee's the one over there operatin' the Wheel of Fortune.'

A gaunt man with grey scraggly hair and sullen eyes paused momentarily in his duties to give Erasimus a look of despair.

'Right. Thanks for clearing that up.' Erasimus scanned the carnival, searching for Jellybean and Caspian.

'Don't menchun it.' The troll shovelled the last heap of dung into the sack, scrawled the words 'Lucky Dip' on the side, slung it over one shoulder and ambled off.

The hotel was a rather grotty affair, three star at best. Still, it was better than a stable. There was even a sign above the door that boasted that particular fact. 'Betr thn a stbl' it read, since several of the letters had fallen off, and no one could be bothered to replace them.

Caspian underpaid the humpless hunchback receptionist, and they retired to their separate rooms. Jellybean's room had clearly been designed with halflings in mind; the walls were covered in pictures of cakes, and a well-stocked larder took up half the space.

He curled up in a foetal position on a bed smaller than he was, and drifted off into a peaceful slumber.

From which he was awoken ten minutes later.

'Change channel!' a loud voice hollered from the room next door.

'Ayiyiyiyiyiyiyiyiyiyiyiyi!' whooped a trio of squeaky voices in response.

Jellybean buried his head beneath the miniscule pillow and tried to block his ears.

'Marshmallow Smoothie!'

'Ayiyiyiyiyiyiyiyiyiyiyiyi!'

After several hours of continuous hollering and whooping, he could bear it no longer. He squeezed into his tiny complimentary bathrobe and slippers, headed out into the hallway and knocked on Caspian's door.

'Door!' a voice yelled from within.

More whoops, and the scrabble of tiny fingers.

The door creaked open and Jellybean shuffled in.

Caspian lay on the bed in his wizardly undergarments, eyes glued to a large crystal ball that had been fixed on the wall opposite the bed. Currently, it was displaying the football.

'Change channel!'

'Ayiyiyiyiyiyiyiyiyi!' The beard pixies scrambled down and pressed a button on the remote, a good two inches from Caspian's hand.

'I'm trying to sleep,' yawned Jellybean.

'Well, you'll never manage it standing around here, will you?' said Caspian, his eyes fixed to the crystal ball. 'Popcorn!'

The beard pixies lassoed a kernel of popcorn from an overflowing bowl on the side and flipped it into his mouth.

'Cheers.' Caspian munched away.

'Could you please keep it down a bit?'

'Dunno about that,' Caspian said. 'One of the pixies is a bit hard of hearing. I wouldn't want him to think I'm prejudiced against his condition.'

'You could always change the channel yourself,' Jellybean said. 'The remote's just there.'

'Nah.' Caspian grinned. 'It'd mean moving. Itchy nose!'

'Ayiyiyiyiyiyiyiyiyi!'

With an exhausted sigh, Jellybean turned his back on the sight of three eager pixies mountaineering up Caspian's face, and left the room.

He padded down the hallway towards Brian's room, and went in. By an uncanny stroke of good fortune, Brian had been given the palatial suite, with a king size bed big enough for several queens. Jellybean found him in the Jacuzzi, with a griffin masseuse working on his shoulders.

'Meeeh…' said Brian softly.

'Sorry,' Jellybean said. 'I didn't realise you had company.'

He approached Erasimus' room opposite, and knocked.

'About bally time!' Erasimus' voice muttered from within. 'Enter!'

Jellybean shuffled in. Erasimus was perched next to the window ledge, looking out at a huge wobbling slab of pink intestines.

'Now look here!' he snapped. 'This is hardly what I had in mind when I asked for a room with a view!' He turned, and saw Jellybean staring at him with bleary eyes. 'Oh. It's you.' His voice softened a moment, and then rose sharply. 'You're supposed to be in bed!'

'The beard pixies were keeping me up,' complained Jellybean, climbing into the large wicker nest in the centre of the room and wrapping himself in its duvet.

'What you need is a rousing bedtime story to send you off to the land of nod,' Erasimus declared.

Jellybean had already fallen asleep.

Erasimus pecked him until he woke up. 'It was the great Baby Boom of '69,' he said, ignoring Jellybean's groans of protest. 'The sun beat down upon us like an ageing yellow adversary. We had a job to do, deliveries to be made, targets to be met. No time for breaks, rations, or toilet stops. Ghastly affair! All around me, delivery birds dropped from the sky, succumbing to the heat. But I was resolute! On I went through the blistering heat, feathers smoking, skin sizzling, on and on and on and –'

Erasimus dozed off mid-sentence.

His shrill warbling snore kept Jellybean awake the rest of the night.

8

Too Much Of A Good Thing

Erasimus wrapped a scarf around his neck, donned his hat and snapped his flying goggles into place. 'All rested and ready to go?'

Jellybean forced open his bloodshot eyes.

'Ah, perhaps not,' Erasimus grimaced. 'I recommend a nice energy-building breakfast, then back to bed for a few hours' extra kip.' He bustled towards the door.

Jellybean yawned. 'Where are you going?'

'Thought I might go down to the golf course and see if I can sink a birdie.'

Jellybean breakfasted alone. Brian was busy having a hoof pedicure, and Caspian was watching Cooking With Magic. From time to time, Jellybean caught sight of the beard pixies, scampering around the table tops as they gathered delicious sugary offerings for their god.

There wasn't much in the way of healthy eating, so Jellybean contented himself with a nourishing bowl of candyfloss soup, chocolate battered donut rings, popcorn drizzled in honey, sugar paper sandwich with brown sugar bread, toffee apple crumble, toffee apple turnover, toffee apple pie with lashings of syrup, and a couple of items from the sweets trolley.

When Erasimus returned several hours later, he found Jellybean manically jumping up and down on his halfling-size bed, yelling 'Bagoolah-Bagoon! Bagoolah-Bagoon! Bagoolah-Bagoon!' at the top of his voice.

'Still awake, eh?' Erasimus scowled.

'I'm –'

Boing!

'– Having –'

Boing!

'– Trouble –'

Boing!

'– Sleeping!'

Boing! Boing! Boing!

Erasimus watched him bounce up and down. His frown softened. 'Oh well, not to worry. I was going to ask if you wouldn't mind staying a bit longer anyway.'

Jellybean came to a sudden stop, and almost toppled off the bed. 'I thought you wanted to leave.'

'Unfortunately, Roger the birdman's gone down with a nasty bout of bird flu, so they've asked me to fill in. Just temporarily, of course.'

'You've joined the Freak Show?' Jellybean said incredulously.

Erasimus puffed out his chest with pride. 'It's not for the money or the glory, dear boy. It's for all those smiles on the children's faces.'

Jellybean stared at him a moment, then went back to his bouncing.

'Since you seem to have rather a lot of excess energy, you might as well work it off at the carnival. And see if that useless wizard wants to accompany you.'

Jellybean found Caspian lying in the same position on his bed, eyes fixed on the crystal ball.

'I'm going to the carnival,' Jellybean said. 'Wanna come?'

'Uh?' grunted Caspian. Popcorn tumbled out of his quivering lips, only to be snagged by tiny lassoes and thrust instantly back in.

'We can play on the Spitting Serpent again, if you like.'

'Shh. Watching Spartacus.'

'But don't you want to –'

'Raise volume!' Caspian commanded.

'Ayiyiyiyi,' whimpered the pixies, red-eyed and exhausted.

Jellybean sighed. He knew exactly how they felt.

After a few goes on the Spitting Serpent, Gnome Catapult, Bedraggled Dragon Racer, Wheezing Warlock, Hook A Horror, Tumbling Hobgoblin, Whack-a-Witch and Catch-a-leper, the sugar rush finally wore off and Jellybean decided to call it a day.

As he walked back through the carnival, he became entangled in a large crowd that had formed outside the House Of Freaks. A garishly dressed goblin wobbled on stilts, hollering through a loudspeaker. 'Roll up! Roll up! Feast your eyes on the fabulous birdman! Marvel at the softness of his feathers! Gasp in horror at the sharpness of his beak! Watch him swoop and soar. See him eat maggots, you'll love it!'

Even Jellybean was caught up in the goblin's enthusiasm. Before he knew what was happening, he'd paid a token and entered.

The catwalk in the centre of the tent heaved with carnival freaks strutting their misshapen stuff. Erasimus circled overhead, performing a dazzling array of loop-de-loops and aerial acrobatics. 'What-ho?' he cawed at the delighted onlookers. 'Pip pip!'

The audience gasped 'Oooh!' 'Aaaah!' and 'Blimey! Roger's act's come on a bit!'

'Mushy maggots!' cried a food vendor as he worked his way through the crowd. 'Feed the bird-man on the wing. Only a token!'

Handful upon handful of live maggots were cast into the air, often missing Erasimus completely and landing on unsuspecting members of the audience.

It was time to make tracks. Jellybean returned to his hotel room, climbed into bed, and fell into a deep blissful sleep.

Apart from a sugar-induced nightmare involving a trio of overzealous dentists attempting to saw off his head, Jellybean slept remarkably well.

He opened his eyes, leapt out of bed, crossed his fingers and thrust them into his bellybutton. A por-tal whummed open, glowing brighter and stronger than ever.

Barely able to contain his excitement, he closed it again and, after brushing his teeth five times, raced off to the House Of Freaks to tell Erasimus the good news.

Erasimus was sitting at a table outside the tent, signing autographs.

'Well, I can hardly leave now, can I?' he breathed, rather testily. 'I'm in the middle of a signing. Wouldn't want to disappoint the fans, eh?'

A chorus of hurrahs went up from the children gathered in the queue, and a couple of boos from the adults forced to queue alongside them.

'But –'

'Come back when I'm less busy.'

Opting to steer clear of the rides and conserve his portal energy, Jellybean entered the Big Top, and watched the afternoon's entertainment. There was precious little of it; the fire breathers cheated by having tiny dragons perched on their tongues, the sword-swallowing elves used toothpicks rather than swords, and the elf-swallowing ogre turned out to not actually be part of the act.

Just as a mysterious troll performer named 'Urgoff the Bean Eater' was preparing to unveil a dynamic new musical act, Jellybean took his leave.

The queue at Erasimus' table had gotten longer.

'Um, I really think we should –' Jellybean began.

'Back of the queue!' yelled a muscular centaur in dark shades, blocking the way.

'But –'

'You pushed in!' the centaur growled, folding his arms across his half-horse, half-human chest. 'Don't think I didn't see you.'

'But I know him.'

'Just because you fed the birdman maggots doesn't make you family,' the centaur snarled. 'To the back! Go on, hop it!'

Jellybean tried again the next day, and the next, but the queue only got longer. Whenever Jellybean joined it, he was greeted with the same response from Erasimus: 'Come back when I'm less busy!'

His only hope rested on Roger the birdman making a speedy recovery, which according to the carnival's resident witchdoctor, was highly unlikely. By his diagnosis, Roger would be dead as a dodo by the end of the month, which, as one kind soul had remarked, was probably the closest Roger ever came to a decent bird impression.

Countless days went by. Occasionally, they were marked by new arrivals. It was easy to spot them; they were the ones covered from head to foot in porridge. Most of them were wrapped in sacrificial robes, and insisted on speaking to management. Apparently, they'd been led to believe the demon's mouth was the gateway to the afterlife. No one had mentioned anything about a carnival.

This sort of thing was clearly a regular occurrence, as the next time Jellybean saw them they were clad in novelty demon-horn hats, and t-shirts that bore the phrase: 'I was sacrificed to D'nabala the Great Spirit God, and all I got was this lousy t-shirt'.

Jellybean sat in his usual place of solace behind the harpy enclosure, staring into the shimmering depths of a portal. The carnival food was starting to weigh heavily on his stomach, and even heavier on his teeth. He craved one of Kleetus' home made delicacies; Swamp weevil stew…Racoon Surprise (the surprise being that the racoon was still alive)…Possum marinated in lard. Tastes that had once repelled him made his mouth water at the thought.

He glanced past the portal, squinting at the twinkling lights of the carnival. He was sick of all the games and rides. He'd played Halfling Bowling so often that all the balls knew him by name.

'Ooh, better luck next time, Jellybean!' the halflings called. And: 'Had this been three pin bowlin', you'da nailed it wi' that one, I reckun!'

The worst part was the loneliness. Whenever he wanted to speak to Erasimus he had to book several days in advance; Brian was busy having countless beauty aids applied to various parts of his body, and could barely manage more than a blissful murmur anymore. As for Caspian, he still hadn't budged an inch from his bed. One time, as Jellybean had trudged down the hotel's hallway, he'd encountered a trio of grim-faced pixies trudging past the other way, with a toilet roll hoisted above their heads.

'You think you've got problems!' one of the pixies had muttered.

Jellybean gave the portal one last lingering look, and closed it again. The last thing he needed was for another demon to rush through and eat him.

'Neat trick,' a voice rumbled behind him. 'You should be in a carnival wiv skills like that.'

Jellybean turned. A troll in orange coveralls grinned back at him.

'Morning, Rockford.'

The troll waved its pitchfork in a cheery fashion. 'All right J.B? Still 'ere then?'

'No one else wants to leave.'

'They're prob'ly under the spell of the carnival,' nodded Rockford. 'All dem bright flashy lights and 'ipnotic noises…It does somethin' to folk. Makes 'em forget their normal life and wanna go round doin' somethin' more glamorous, like, I dunno, shovellin' dung or somethin'.' It slopped its sack before Jellybean. 'Lucky dip?'

'No thanks,' Jellybean said. 'I've seen what you've been putting in there.'

'Ah c'mon…' The troll beamed. 'Yer never know when yer luck's about to change.' It rattled the sack under Jellybean's nose in an enticing fashion. The overwhelming reek of manure filled his nostrils.

Jellybean sighed. Every day, the same old routine…

He screwed his eyes tight and plunged an arm into the sack, all the way up to the shoulder. Perhaps this time things would be different; perhaps this time he'd find something that hadn't dropped out of a harpy's bottom.

The contents of the sack were soft and warm beneath his fingers, which wasn't necessarily a good thing. He rummaged around under the gleeful eye of the troll, exploring the bag's nooks and crannies. Just when he was about to give up, his fingers brushed against something reassuringly solid. He gripped hold of the item and dragged it out of the bag.

It was a half-eaten boot; not just any boot, but the very one Caspian had flung through the portal at the Screaming Heebie-Jeebie.

'Brian's favourite boot…' he murmured. He hugged it to his chest, staining his t-shirt with manure. It was a little slice of home.

An idea began to take shape in his mind. It spread out, gathering strength until it became a fully-grown escape strategy. It was going to be risky, and if it backfired he could lose his friends for good.

'Thanks, Rockford!' Jellybean cried, as he dashed off, swinging the boot by its laces. 'You're the greatest!'

The troll waved him off, then turned and frowned at the sack. 'How'd that get in there?' it muttered.

9

Escape!

Three days passed. Jellybean finished his prepa-
rations. After one hundred and seventy two
return trips through the portal, he'd found what he
was looking for.

Finding a planet with a chemists close enough to
the portal proved tricky. In the end, he'd had to
settle for chicken soup from a remote convenience
store in the Shasticon Brengali cluster. He was their
first customer in more than fifty two million years,
and by way of celebrating they'd let him have the
soup for free (the blue-skinned manager had wanted
Jellybean to pose for a few publicity photos, but
after Jellybean had politely explained that demons
might rush through his bellybutton portal and eat
everyone, they were suddenly rather keen for him to
leave).

Jellybean had an early night to ensure he'd be
ready for departure in the morning. Apart from
embarking on a stealthy trip to Caspian's room, he
experienced the best night's sleep he'd had since
arriving at the carnival.

At eight in the morning, a knock on the door
roused him from his slumber. Erasimus was outside,
fully dressed and ready to go.

He clapped his wings together. 'Pip pip! Tally-ho. Time waits for no whatsit!'

Jellybean raised inquisitive eyebrows. 'Haven't you got fans to entertain?'

Erasimus shuffled his webbed feet. 'Bit of a sore point, actually. Less said the better, eh?'

'I'd like to hear more,' Jellybean grinned.

'I was ousted by a rascally old rotter named Roger,' Erasimus said bitterly.

'He got better?'

'Yes. Some bally rascal fed him chicken soup.'

'The best cure for all illnesses…' Jellybean murmured.

'Chicken soup of all things!' Erasimus squawked in distaste. 'For a birdman, that's practically cannibalism. Of course, now all the kiddies are eager to see who he eats next. The scoundrel even had the nerve to ask if I wouldn't mind becoming part of his new act and letting him gnaw on my wings.'

Jellybean's glow of satisfaction dulled. 'What did you tell him?'

'I'm afraid I can't repeat that in the presence of a child. Suffice to say, I quit on the spot!' Erasimus puffed out his feathers. 'After all, if a bird hasn't got his dignity, what has he got?'

'My beard!' Caspian's voice screamed from down the hall. 'Someone's stolen my beard!'

Jellybean and Erasimus dashed down the hallway towards Caspian's room.

'What seems to be the –' Erasimus stopped abruptly inside the doorway, and stared in horror at the mass of wizardly blubber that lay on the bed, folds of fat trembling rhythmically. 'Good god, man, you're enormous!'

'Never mind that,' Caspian sobbed. 'Someone shaved off my beard whilst I slept!'

'You had a beard?' Erasimus said. 'I never even noticed.'

'It was a thing of wonder.' Caspian's bare chin trembled uncontrollably. Beneath it, several more chins joined in the mourning ceremony. 'And now it's gone…all gone.'

'Oh, well.' Erasimus patted him gently on a pink wobbly bit that was probably his shoulder. 'You can always grow another one.'

Caspian instantly stopped sobbing, though his chins went on wobbling. 'Are you mad? It'd take me months! Besides…the pixies…my precious little beard pixies have left me.' The tears began to flow again.

Jellybean had to grit his teeth to stop himself from mentioning that not only had the pixies cheered whilst he'd shaved off Caspian's beard, but they'd also provided the shaving foam.

'Change the channel…' Caspian called in a weak voice. 'Please…someone…change the channel…'

'Do it yourself, you lazy scoundrel,' Erasimus snapped. 'The remote's next to you.'

Caspian rolled his head with pitiful slowness. His podgy fingers crept towards the remote. Beads of sweat broke out on his forehead. 'Muscles…too weak. Somebody…fetch me a pixie!'

'You've had enough pixies to last a lifetime,' Erasimus chided, staring at Caspian's midriff. 'The best thing we can do is get you out of this ghastly place, and find a planet populated by fitness fanatics. I only pray the portal's wide enough.'

'I'll get your robe,' Jellybean said, anxious to offset the twinges of guilt by doing something helpful. He retrieved the robe from off the back of a chair, and handed it to Caspian.

With great effort, Caspian hauled his vast frame to its feet and attempted to force his massive arms into the tiny sleeves. Within seconds, the robe hung off him in tatters.

'That won't do at all!' Erasimus declared. 'A man can't travel the universe in his undergarments. Wouldn't be proper.'

Caspian plunged a hand into the pocket of the shredded robe. 'I just hope the stability of the wormhole hasn't been damaged,' he muttered, 'or it's curtains for this universe.' Sweat dripped off him as he rummaged around with growing desperation.

Erasimus nodded. 'Ah, I see. Got some sort of slim-fast device in there, eh? Something that'll strip the weight from your bones in seconds?'

Caspian drew out his hand. Clutched in his palm was a large dollop of cold, congealed porridge. With a sigh of relief, he thrust it into his mouth.

Jellybean and Erasimus watched in revulsion.

'I think it might be time to admit that you have a teensy bit of an eating problem,' Erasimus said, averting his eyes as Caspian chewed.

'Uhhhr?' said Caspian, shovelling in another handful of porridge.

'Good god, man, you're eating porridge from your pockets! Could it possibly be any worse?'

'Got sweets in it.' Caspian crunched away merrily.

'Oh, well that's perfectly all right then.' Erasimus rolled his eyes. 'I'm sure a few extra calories'll do you the world of good.'

'Not normal sweets. Tailors' Toffees.'

Suddenly there was a noise like a tiny firework popping, and a small silk thread burst out of Caspian's chest, followed by another and another and another. Pop! Pop! Pop! Pop! His whole body was riddled with tiny silken explosions. The threads wrapped themselves around Caspian's body, cocooning him, until he was covered from head to foot.

A heartbeat later, the silk cocoon split open. Caspian stood before them in a perfectly fitting robe and body armour, looking incredibly smug. 'I needed an outfit for the more portly gentleman,' he explained. He waddled towards the mirror, and admired his reflection. It was a struggle for the mirror to fit him all in.

After licking the palm of his hand and smoothing his ruffled hair back a bit, he gunned his fingers at his image. 'Heh. Still got it!'

Jellybean was suddenly aware how grubby his own clothing looked when placed next to Caspian's sparkling new armour and shimmering robe. Caspian must've noticed him staring, as he dropped something into the palm of his hand. 'I promise not to steal your pigs,' he said, with a wink.

Jellybean looked down. His hand contained a large dollop of porridge, with a Tailors' Toffee lodged in the centre. 'How come that robe's also got porridge in its pockets?'

'Didn't I explain about my pockets earlier?'

'Not very well,' mumbled Erasimus.

'It's all shareware technology, right?' Caspian said. 'Thanks to the wormhole contained inside, I'm not just putting a hand in my pocket, but into the pockets of every Techno Mage in the entire universe. I get access to their stuff, and they get access to mine. It's a fair system.'

Erasimus' eyes narrowed. 'Hang on a bally moment! You mean to say none of that stuff you traded in for carnival tokens was actually yours?'

'I think the walnut was mine,' Caspian said. 'Otherwise, no.'

Jellybean eagerly unwrapped the sweet. 'What type is it?'

'Self-Styled. Absolutely anything you can imagine. A suit of armour, dragon hide, tank top, anything. So make sure you think carefully now,' Caspian warned. 'After all, it's hard to save the universe when you're dressed in a monkey suit. I should know. I tried it once.'

Jellybean popped the sweet in his mouth, closed his eyes, and tried to picture the far off kingdoms he'd seen in his dreams. Richly dressed merchants, and chainmail-clad warriors swam into focus, waving for his attention.

'Silk pantaloons, my lord?' a smarmy merchant grovelled. 'Impress the girls! Confound the boys!'

'Kraken-skin shirt?' rumbled a battle-hardened mercenary. 'Turns aside the sharpest of blades!'

Just as Jellybean was homing in on a particularly dazzling pair of curly shoes that had caught his eye, Kleetus' ragged dungaree-clad form stomped across his field of vision.

'Jellybean!' he yelled, fixing him with a mean glare. 'Get back here and finish your chores!'

Before Jellybean could dispel the image, he heard the pop pop popping of silk, and held his breath as millions of tiny little threads tightened around his body.

With a loud 'R-r-riiip!' the cocoon split open, and Jellybean burst out, clad in a brand new perfectly fitting outfit. He opened his eyes to see Caspian and Erasimus staring at him with distaste.

'Chequered red shirt, and dungarees?'

Jellybean smiled weakly. 'I've always wanted a pair that fit. Look, it's even got a little flap in the front for easier bellybutton access.'

'You can take the hillbilly out of the country...' Caspian sighed.

Jellybean slapped a hand roughly against his forehead. 'I almost forgot Brian!' He rushed back to his room and rattled a half-eaten, manure-encrusted boot. 'Brian!' he hollered. 'Dinner's ready.'

Brian's door burst open and the goat charged out, hair still in rollers and eyelashes freshly crimped.

'Meeeeeh!' he cried in joy. Taking the boot tenderly between his teeth, he shook it, spreading manure in every direction. Within moments, he was restored to his grubby self.

Jellybean flicked a few specks of manure from his new dungarees and tickled Brian behind the ears. 'Good lad.'

'Can we go now?' asked Erasimus.

Jcllybcan nodded. 'I'll go tell the others to get ready.' He clomped off down the hallway, admiring his brand new curly shoes.

Caspian strode out, scratching his corpulent scalp. 'Others?' he said.

10

King Caspian

Mad King Numbles stood at the window of his castle, gazing out over the heads of his loyal subjects.

Most of the heads were on spikes. Hence, his recent 'I'm actually all right once you get to know me' speech hadn't gone down at all well. Several people had dared to snigger. Others had muttered 'a likely bloomin' story!' One thing had led to another and, quicker than the king could cry 'off with their heads!' the guillotine was in need of another good scrub.

The king sighed. That was the trouble with people these days; they didn't take the time to consider *his* feelings. It took a great deal of effort being a ruthless tyrant; all those hours spent plotting and scheming, trying to keep up with the latest trends. Only last month he'd invented a dozen new ways to torture people, just to add a bit of variety to their lives, but did anyone bother to thank him? No.

All they'd said was 'Argh!'

Well, King Numbles had had enough! He was getting too old for this sort of thing. The constant peasant revolts and assassination attempts were starting to annoy him. It was time for a new approach – a new way of thinking.

He tore his eyes away from the view, and strode across his gnome-skin rug. 'It's time,' he declared in a bold, decisive voice, 'to try being nice to people!'

Someone sniggered outside the door of his chambers. He threw it open, and peered out at the guards on either side. The one on the left hurriedly attempted to bury his head in his suit of armour.

'You find something amusing?' the king enquired.

'Not any more, sire,' Lefty said weakly, the colour draining from his square-jawed features. 'I'll go cut my head off, shall I? Save you the bother.' He pulled out his sword and drew it back, ready for a swipe.

'Oh, put it away, for goodness' sake!' the king snapped. 'This is exactly the sort of thing I'm trying to get away from.'

'Strike a leper!' the other guard exclaimed. 'You mean you're serious about this "nice" thing?'

King Numbles turned his icy gaze upon the guard. 'You doubt I'm capable of changing my ways?'

'Yes, I mean no, I…uh…' The guard stammered himself into silence.

'It's not just the way you act, sire,' said Lefty, glancing pointedly at the king's gnome-skin waistcoat and matching gnome-skin accessories, 'it's the way you dress. I mean, it's hardly likely to win any votes of confidence from the kingdom's gnome community, is it?'

The king soothed his wrinkled forehead. 'But I like gnomes,' he said. 'They're comfy.'

Lefty jammed a tiny Puff Dragon in the corner of his mouth, and took a long drag. 'All I'm sayin' is it's gonna be hard to convince folk what a thoroughly pleasant bloke you are, when you're parading around wearin' some poor fellow's aunty.'

'Hmm…you may have a point,' said the king. 'I'll raise the subject with my adviser when he – ah! Speak of the devil.'

'Sorry I'm late, sire. Sorry! Sorry!' A tall, perilously thin man with a sharp bony body rushed up the stairs, and bowed low before the king, scraping his griffin-feathered hat along the ground. 'I only pray this small token of fealty will compensate for my tardiness.' He straightened up and held out a delicately wrapped gift box in the palm of a bandaged hand.

'Oh, Clarence,' the king sighed, waving the unopened gift away. 'Not another finger.'

'Not enough?' the king's adviser squealed. 'Say no more, sire. I'll hack off a toe. Two toes…the entire foot!' He beckoned Lefty to hand over his sword.

'Actually, I think you'll find he's not doing that sort of thing any more,' said Lefty.

A bead of sweat rolled off the tip of Clarence's pointed nose. 'Serves me right!' he wailed, falling to his knees. 'I've failed you for the last time, sire. It's off to the gallows for me, or worse…the Pit of Livid Monkeys!'

'As a matter of fact,' said Lefty, trying to keep a straight face, 'he's decided to try being nice.'

Clarence stopped bawling, and looked baffled.

King Numbles' features contorted into a variety of unpleasant expressions as he tried to remember how to smile. 'Out with the old, and what have you,' he said, grinning like an angry Rottweiler.

'I'm not sure I understand, sire,' said Clarence, as the king helped him to his feet. 'Is this some sort of joke? If it is, then may I commend you on your cruel sense of humour.'

'No joke, Clarence,' King Numbles sighed. 'All this cutting people's heads off and whatnot, it's a bit excessive, isn't it? I mean, at the end of the day, what does it really achieve?'

'Heads on spikes, sire,' said Lefty keenly. 'Can't go wrong with heads on spikes.'

'Better than hanging baskets, if you want my opinion,' said Righty. 'They don't need watering. Low maintenance, always a bonus.'

'But people look at me like I'm some sort of raving lunatic. It's most discomforting!'

'Very good, sire,' said Clarence. 'I shall make an announcement. From this day forth, anyone caught looking at our beloved king without permission shall have their eyes put through with a red-hot poker. Or perhaps a cold one. Whichever hurts most.'

The guards hurriedly averted their eyes. Clarence followed suit.

'Stop that nonsense!' snapped the king, his face reddening. 'I'm going to be nice, even if it kills me.'

Clarence risked a glance upwards. 'Forgive me for saying so, sire, but royalty does not do nice. Pleasantly amused by a burning beggar, or small child who's fallen into a snake pit, perhaps, but certainly not nice.'

The king stormed back into his chamber and slammed the door. 'I need your support on this one, Clarence!' he hollered.

Clarence edged in through the door, anxious to avoid the tyrant's wrath. Inside, he found the king staring out the window, deep in thought.

'What I really need is to wipe the glum looks off those peasants' faces,' King Numbles mused.

The two guards crept in after Clarence, and took up their posts.

'How about a public flogging?' suggested Lefty.

'I was thinking more along the lines of some sort of festivity.'

Clarence snapped his fingers. 'A hanging! They always draw a crowd.'

'Clarence, please…'

'Witch burnin's are popular, sire,' said Righty.

'Not with witches, they're not.'

Clarence closed his eyes, and took a ramble through his mind, ignoring the dastardly plots and evil schemes that waved for his attention. He pushed past into his childhood, searching for Happier Times and Fond Memories. And there it was, parading past like a noisy overdressed peacock…

'How about…a carnival, sire?' he said cautiously.

King Numbles' features did another contorting act, and for a moment Clarence thought he was about to go for his throat. Instead, the king reached out and patted him warmly on the shoulder. 'Excellent idea!' he declared, grinning like a rabid badger. 'Just the sort of radical New Age thinking I'm looking for. A bit of fun…a bit of joviality. That'll show those ugly peasants how much I care about them. Yes,' he said, waving his beefy arms around in excitement, 'a carnival with clowns, tumbling dwarves and fire breathers who don't immediately set themselves alight in an attempt to impress me.' He turned to the guards and boomed: 'Find me a carnival act!'

Lefty scratched the back of his head nervously, staring out at the rows of beheaded clowns beyond the window. 'Just one slight snag,' he said. 'You had us execute all the carnival folk only last week.'

The king deflated like a hedgehog's balloon. 'I hope I had a jolly good reason.'

'Oh yes, a very just reason. Very just indeed.'

'What was it, man?'

'Didn't like the height of one of their dwarves, sire. Said he was two inches too tall.'

'We shortened him up, all right,' said Righty, making a cutting motion across his neck.

'Surely you could round up a few beggars and get them to perform tricks?' the king said, his voice wavering. 'Juggling, and so forth.'

'I should imagine that would be a rather complicated affair,' said Lefty, 'since you had us remove their hands.'

'On the plus side,' Righty added hurriedly, 'begging's down.'

King Numbles rested his elbows on the windowsill. 'That's that, then,' he said. 'I tried to be nice. I tried to do what's right for the people. Sometimes I don't know why I even –'

Suddenly, a shining blue portal whummed opened in the courtyard below. The king watched in amazement as a procession of jugglers stepped out, followed by goblins on stilts, acrobatic halflings, fire breathers, a birdman, a magician of enormous girth, fortune-telling witches, misfortune-telling warlocks, toothpick-swallowing elves, elf-swallowing ogres, a small child in his dungarees, a troll with melodic flatulence, a goat…

As he gazed upon the incredible spectacle, King Numbles' features contorted one last time, and finally…finally, he remembered how to smile. 'Clarence?' he chimed, in a voice as joyous as a thousand angels singing. 'Fetch me my horse!'

'I still say this is an extremely bad idea,' said Erasimus. 'Letting all these carnival folk loose on an unsuspecting planet. No good'll come of it, you mark my words.'

'I couldn't just leave them trapped in a demon's belly,' said Jellybean.

'Never mind that now,' said Caspian. 'We've only got a few minutes before we need to close the portal. Is everybody here?' He inspected the large carnival procession that had shuffled, blinking, into the daylight.

'We could do a quick headcount,' suggested Jellybean.

'I think perhaps it's best we don't,' said Erasimus, surveying the castle walls.

Caspian followed his eyes to the strange lumpy shapes mounted on spikes all around them. 'Tsh!' he said. 'Someone certainly has a flair for the dramatic.' He turned back to the carnival folk, and beamed. 'Anyway, here we are. Your new home.'

A few disapproving mutters rippled through the carnival's ranks.

Rockford the troll pushed to the front and cleared its throat, making the battlements shake. 'I think I speak for all of us,' it rumbled, 'when I say we're probably just going to leave it.'

'But…but…' stammered Jellybean.

'Thanks for tryin' though, kid.' It pushed back through the crowd.

'But you live inside a demon,' said Jellybean.

'Could be worse, eh?' said Rockford. 'At least I don't live here.' The troll stepped back into the portal and vanished. One by one, the carnival folk followed.

'There's gratitude!' muttered Erasimus.

'Hold on,' said Caspian, adjusting the magnification level on his glasses. 'Someone's approaching.'

A massive black war stallion thundered across the cobblestones, from the castle keep. Its rider was a burly, bull-necked brute of a man; skin wrinkled and discoloured, like a corpse left to rot in the sun. Upon his head he wore a gruesome crown made from the concertinaed bodies of a dozen golden fairies. Behind him trailed a blood-red cloak stitched together from hundreds of glum-faced gnomes, one of whom was still holding a fishing rod, though his fishing days were over.

'I don't like the look of him,' said Caspian, as the rider drew closer. 'Looks a bit evil.'

'He seems to be shouting and waving a lot,' Erasimus remarked. 'What on Hotchpotch is wrong with the man?'

'You know what?' said Caspian, as the stallion tore up the cobblestones. 'I don't think he's going to stop.'

They dodged as the rider galloped past.

'Wait! Please! Come back!' King Numbles cried, as the last of the carnival folk stepped through the portal. 'I'm actually all right once you get to know me!' The horse bore its rider onwards through the shimmering depths of the portal.

Jellybean poked a finger into his bellybutton, and closed the portal behind the rider.

'What a ghastly man,' breathed Erasimus.

'Certainly had a thing against gnomes,' said Caspian.

From out of the grimy dwellings around them, grubby-faced peasants started to emerge.

'Oh dear,' Erasimus said, as the peasants grew in number.

'Sorry!' Caspian offered. 'I do hope he wasn't anyone important.'

A cry rang out from the battlements. 'The king is dead! The king is dead!'

'No he isn't,' Caspian insisted, sheltering Jellybean from the advancing mob. 'He's at a carnival. Probably having the time of his life.'

A trumpet blew. 'Rejoice! Rejoice! The tyrant is dead!'

The crowd whooped and cheered.

'Tyrant, eh?' Caspian murmured. 'Well, that's different then.' He stepped forward, hoisting a thumb at his chest. 'It was me. I did it. Caspian Thrall...the man who killed the king. I accept full responsibility for this most heinous of crimes. Do with me as you will!' He held out his hands to be cuffed.

A peasant leant forward and shook one of them. 'Well done! Good work. I always said he was a wrong 'un.'

A burly blacksmith slapped Caspian roughly on the back. 'Got what was comin' to him, if yer want my opinion.'

Jellybean, Erasimus and Brian were gradually edged out of the circle as more and more peasants rushed to shake Caspian by the hand.

'The nerve of the man!' Erasimus muttered.

Caspian thrust out his chest, almost knocking several peasants off their feet. 'Caspian Thrall, slayer of evil tyrants!' he declared. His eyes scanned the crowd for anyone vaguely resembling a musician, eventually settling on a man in a straw hat who was eating cream cheese out of a lute. 'If there be any bards present,' he said, giving the man a knowing wink, 'feel free to compose a ballad about my exploits. You might want to chuck in a few extra damsels here and there, and perhaps a dragon or two.'

'Hooray for our saviour! Hurrah!' called Lefty from the window above, keen for the mob to know which side of the bread his loyalty was buttered.

The crowd of peasants grunted and strained as they attempted to lift their conquering hero off the ground. It took six people to complete the procedure, and even then they only managed to get him as far as their ankles.

'Can we put him down now?' said a weak voice.

This plan was greeted with much enthusiasm, and they returned Caspian rather abruptly to the ground. After helping him up, patting his back and shaking his hand a few more times, an air of uncertainty descended on the crowd.

'Hang about,' said a peasant, voicing everyone's concern, 'who's going to run the kingdom now?'

The peasants exchanged glances. They whispered conspiratorially among themselves, and as one, turned towards Caspian. They had big toothless smiles on their faces.

'Sorry to be a party pooper,' Erasimus said sternly, 'but I'm afraid we really ought to be –'

'Paid position, is it?' Caspian smoothly interjected.

The peasants nodded.

'Now hang on a bally moment!'

'Royal treasury overflowing with gold and rare gems?' Caspian continued, ignoring Erasimus' protests.

More nods.

Caspian smiled so widely that he threatened to decapitate himself. 'Very well, I accept.'

Erasimus soared over the crowd, and dropped to land beside Caspian. 'We don't have time for this,' he squawked. 'We're already behind schedule. We have to find Hotchpotch.'

'It's not like being king's a full-time job,' Caspian said, giving the crowd the royal wave. 'All I need do is pop back from time to time, kiss a few babies, and everyone's happy.'

'There's no going back,' Erasimus snapped. 'Our young Navigator doesn't know how!'

Caspian leant in close. 'Yes, but they don't know that do they?' he hissed. He turned back towards his subjects. 'Would one of you folks be good enough to point me in the direction of the treasury? I've just got to make a, uh, quick inspection.'

The peasants shuffled their feet. An old woman with a face like a shrivelled prune raised a hand.

Caspian huffed in irritation. 'Yes? What is it?'

'What are your views on taxes, Yer Majisty?' asked the old woman.

'Never seen the point, to be honest,' said Caspian, playing it safe. 'Now, as I was saying –'

'How about crime?' asked a shifty-looking man with a scar down the side of his face. 'What do you think about crime?'

'Dead against it,' said Caspian. 'Unless you're a criminal, in which case I'm for it,' he added promptly. 'Now, I really must –'

'In that case, how are you gonna lower crime without raisin' the taxes?' enquired the old woman.

'Yeah, or raise crime, without lowerin' the taxes?' said the shifty-looking man.

The crowd stared expectantly at Caspian.

He started to sweat. 'Ooh, yes, it is a bit of a balancing act isn't it? Er…' He looked around for assistance.

'That goat ate my turnip!' yelled a vegetable stall owner, pointing a finger at Brian. 'I demand justice!'

'Meeeeh!' said Brian as he chewed.

Caspian scratched the back of his scalp. 'Well, now, I'm sure we can reach some sort of compensatory –'

'Off with his head!' chanted the crowd, closing in around the goat.

'Get yore hands off my goat!' Jellybean yelled.

Erasimus took to the sky, avoiding a clumsily hurled pitchfork. 'Perhaps now would be a fitting time to abdicate the throne, Your Majesty?'

'You're just jealous because you don't have a kingdom,' Caspian grumbled. He heard the familiar 'whumm' of a portal opening. 'Hey! Wait for me!'

He inspected the wall of peasants blocking his path, and then launched himself at it. Even under the force of his immense girth, it failed to give.

'Will you get a bally move on?' Erasimus called.

Caspian hoisted himself up onto the black-smith's broad shoulders, and ran full pelt across the crowd's heads, using them like ugly round stepping-stones. Grubby fingers clawed at him as he ran.

He could see the top of the portal clearly now; Brian had already made swift his escape. Jellybean leapt in after him. Erasimus loop-de-looped one last time, then swooped through.

Caspian reached the edge of the straining crowd, and with a victorious cry, belly-flopped towards the portal.

With a sickening crunch, he slapped into the cobblestones.

When he opened his eyes, the portal was gone.

11

Dinner For One

*C*lick! *Whuuuuuuuuuumph!*
'No. Too pink.'
Click! Whuuuuuuuuumph!
'No. Too mauve.'
Click! Whuuuuuuuuumph!
'No. Too splook.'

Jellybean's finger hovered over his bellybutton. 'Splook?'

'That's right,' Erasimus said, casting a critical eye over the landscape. 'Far too splook for my liking. Absolutely brimming with splook, if you want my opinion.'

Jellybean examined the planet's discoloured surface. 'Looks more sort of yellowy-green to me.'

Erasimus rolled his eyes in exasperation. 'That's what I said – splook. Anyway, point is we're on the wrong bally planet again.'

Jellybean poked a finger in his bellybutton, and gave it another go.

Click! Whuuuuuuuuumph!

'Aha!' Erasimus cried. 'A dingy, sludgy browny sort of colour. Much more promising.'

They slogged through the mud, and approached a ramshackle cluster of dwellings masquerading as a town.

'This is it!' Erasimus enthused. 'This is the one. I can feel it in my feathers!'

'I dunno,' Jellybean said, looking around at the unfriendly faces that peered through crooked doors and misshapen windows. 'I don't remember the folk in Caspian's kingdom being quite so green.'

'Perhaps it was something they ate?' Erasimus reasoned. 'Look! See? They've got a castle and everything.'

Jellybean squinted off into the distance. 'But that's green as well.'

Erasimus bustled up to a grubby market trader who was herding live melons into a cage. 'Excuse me, my young melon wrangler –'

'*Aaaaah!*' the trader screamed, pointing a trembling finger. *'Demons!'*

He ran off at full pelt, scattering fruit in every direction.

'What? Where?' Erasimus glanced behind him. 'Could've sworn we closed the portal.'

'I think he meant us,' Jellybean said.

A dishevelled priest gibbered uncontrollably as they passed.

'It's all right,' Erasimus beamed, 'we're not demons.' He unfurled a wing towards Brian. 'He, for example, is a goat.'

'*Aaaaah!*' wailed the priest. 'Goats!'

Panic-stricken feet stampeded through the mud. Doors slammed. Windows were hurriedly barred.

Somewhere far across the fields, an alarm bell tolled.

Erasimus clicked his beak thoughtfully. 'This might come as a bit of a surprise,' he said, 'but I'm not altogether convinced this is the right planet either.'

'We'll never find Caspian at this rate.'

'Perhaps it's for the best,' Erasimus said. 'I mean, it's not like he actually did anything useful. Good riddance to bad magic, that's what I say.'

'You're the one who left him there,' Jellybean muttered.

Erasimus casually preened beneath a wing. 'I think you'll find you're in charge of the navigating, dear fellow.'

'You told me to close the portal, before he was through.'

'Well, you should've been paying more attention,' Erasimus sniffed. 'Besides, you have to admit, that statue did bear an uncanny resemblance.'

'It was a boulder!'

'Same difference.' Erasimus shrugged. 'It was big and round and didn't have a beard. What more do you want?'

'I want my wizard back,' Jellybean said firmly.

'Oh, very well. I'm sure we can squeeze in a couple more planets before suppertime.' Erasimus' stomach grumbled disapprovingly. 'That bally wizard better appreciate this.'

'Beeeeeeeeep! Target locked!'

Caspian's eyes flitted down to the portal tracker flashing away beside him, and then rose to survey the vast mounds of mouth-watering dishes laid out on a seemingly endless stretch of table; glazed Ninnygog, minced Manticore, Sasquatch stew, barbequed Basilisk, curried Troll tongues, pickled eye of the Beholder, battered Mermaid in a seaweed sauce...

He licked his lips and slobbered. Truly a banquet fit for a king!

The dining room door clattered open, and Clarence's frail figure stalked in. He jogged the full two hundred metres from one end of the table to the other and arrived out of breath. 'I bring troubling news from the kitchen, sire,' he wheezed, collapsing at Caspian's feet.

'No ketchup then?' Caspian grumbled.

'Alas!' Clarence wailed. 'The cook does not know the formula. Though he's quietly confident that with the aid of a few supple gnomes, he might be able to –'

'No, no, it's fine,' Caspian said hurriedly. 'I'll muddle through.' He reached for a plate of drumsticks and recoiled as his robe burst into flames.

'Might I recommend using the tongs provided, sire?' suggested Clarence, dousing the blaze with a flagon of Boggit Breath. 'The Phoenix tends to be a touch on the hot side.'

'Just as well I'm a big fan of spicy foods.' Caspian grasped the edge of the plate with the tongs, and tipped the entire contents into his mouth. His cheeks reddened, eyes streamed, and a jet of flames erupted from each nostril. 'Ahhh,' he croaked. 'That's the stuff!'

'*Beeeeeep! Target Locked!*' urged the portal tracker.

'Oh, give it a rest,' Caspian muttered, draping a napkin over it. 'Interrupting a man's dinner…' His eyes went for another stroll around the table, and spied out an ancient cauldron, covered in occult markings. 'A spot of soup next, I think.'

'Don't forget your earmuffs, sire,' Clarence cautioned.

'Why? What's it going to do – sing at me?' He lifted the cauldron's lid, and was hit full blast by an ear-splitting wail that rattled the teeth around in his skull. Dishes levitated off the table and whirled past overhead, shattering against the wall. He leant on the lid with all his girth, and forced it back down.

'Shrieking Banshee soup,' yelled Clarence, removing his fingers from his ears. 'An acquired taste, at best.'

'Then I, my dear fellow, intend to acquire it!' boasted Caspian. He donned the royal earmuffs, lifted the lid and braced for impact. As he inched closer to the cauldron's contents, the fat folds of his face rippled magnificently. Liquid bubbled and seethed, swirling round like a whirlpool. Hideous ghostly images formed on its surface. '*Turn baaaaack!*' they mouthed. *'Turn baaaaack before it's tooo laaaaaaaate!'*

Before he could react, soup sprayed upwards in one enormous ectoplasmic stream that lifted him off his chair and pinned him against the ceiling.

'Would you like me to fetch you a priest, sire?' Clarence hollered from his hiding place under the table.

'No!' Caspian gurgled. 'I refuse to be bested...*glub!*...by a bowl of haunted soup!' He opened his mouth wide, and sucked with all his might.

When Clarence finally deemed it safe to emerge, he found a thoroughly drenched Caspian sprawled out next to an empty cauldron, daintily mopping his brow with a hunk of bread.

'Damn fine soup,' he commented.

And so culinary carnage ensued, as Caspian battled his way through ruthless hordes of Vampire Parsnips, Suicide Scorpions, Cannibalistic Clams and Exploding Artichokes.

One by one the deadly dishes succumbed to his vast appetite, until there was nothing left but gristle, bone and a solitary bowl of psychic spuds which had telepathically persuaded Caspian to eat everything else but them.

'Most impressive, sire,' Clarence said, eyeing the empty plates. 'Even King Numbles at his most ravenous could rarely manage a whole Kraken.'

'Hah!' scoffed Caspian. ''Twas little more than a kipper!' He expelled an almighty belch fit to rival the Shrieking Banshees for volume, and dabbed the corners of his mouth with a napkin.

'Beeeeeep! Target locked!'

With a sigh, Caspian scooped up the portal trackcr in his podgy fingers, and struggled to his feet. 'Right,' he said. 'I'm off then.'

'Very good, sire.' Clarence bowed low. 'I shall have the royal bedchambers prepared immediately.'

'Not off to bed, Clarence. Off to a different planet.' Caspian jabbed the portal tracker's big green button. 'Got to see a boy about a goat, know what I mean?'

'Destination accepted,' declared the device. *'Portal piggy-back in ten seconds.'*

'Y-y-y-you're leaving, sire?' Clarence stammered. 'B-but you're king!'

Caspian licked a gem-encrusted fork clean, and stuffed it into his pocket. 'Yes, well I'll be sure to pop in if ever I'm passing by this way again.'

Clarence fell to his knees and pawed helplessly as Caspian's feet. 'What about your royal duties?' he whined. 'There are beggars to be flogged... gnomes to persecute...'

'That all sounds like hilariously good fun and everything,' Caspian said, shaking off his adviser. 'But I've already sworn allegiance to the Navigator. Can't leave Jellybean fending for himself whilst there are portal demons on the rampage. I've got responsibilities...commitments...'

A procession of smartly dressed elves bustled in through the door, carrying trays heaped with a staggering assortment of cakes, chocolates, buns, biscuits, treacles, trifles, mousses, and meringues.

Caspian's finger automatically jabbed the portal tracker's big red button.

'Destination cancelled.'

'Then again,' he added, easing his bulk back into the seat. 'If there's *dessert*...'

12

Lost Property

Jellybean tumbled out through a portal no bigger than himself, and landed face down in an enormous pile of unwashed socks.

Struggling to his feet, he peered out over the edge. The bottom was nowhere in sight, shrouded in a thick layer of mist. Around him, mountains of mundane items loomed out of the haze; towering heaps of forks, teaspoons, earrings, paper clips, car keys, lottery tickets, jigsaw pieces, and loose change.

Brian stood atop a heap of biros, crunching noisily away.

'Probably best you don't eat those, lad,' Jellybean warned. 'They'll turn your spit a funny colour.'

'Bleeeeh!' said Brian, poking out an alarmingly blue tongue.

A thump and a squawk signalled Erasimus' arrival. Jellybean looked up to discover the unfortunate stork was wedged at the waist in the portal's tiny opening.

'I say!' he spluttered. 'That's rather bad form! Closing a portal before a chap's entirely through. If you're trying to make a point about that ghastly Caspian affair –'

'It closed itself, actually,' Jellybean said, trying to suppress a smile at the thought of the archaic stork's rear-end dangling helplessly in the depths of space.

'Finally ran out of juice, eh? Can't say I'm surprised.' Erasimus wriggled away, attempting to corkscrew his body through the gap. 'Any chance of a hand, dear boy?'

Jellybean gave his bellybutton a poke. The portal constricted.

'Ow!' Erasimus winced. 'Other way! Other way!'

Jellybean tried again.

The portal tightened further.

'Will you leave that blasted bellybutton alone?' Erasimus growled. 'Find a rope or something.'

Jellybean scrabbled around in the heap of socks, looking for a rope. No matter how deep he dug, all he turned up were more socks. Finally, an idea hit him: he'd use *socks.*

He knotted several dozen together and formed a lasso.

'Just be careful where you put that noose,' Erasimus urged, as Jellybean swirled the lasso around his head. 'I don't want to end up with it wrapped around my ne-mpffffff!' The noose closed tight around his beak.

Jellybean tossed the other end towards Brian. 'That's it, lad,' he encouraged, as Brian took hold of the line of socks in his mouth. 'Pull!'

Brian started to chew.

'No, not chew. Pull. *Pull!*'

As Erasimus' neck was wrenched violently forwards, his eyes bulged.

'Good work, Brian!' Jellybean hollered. 'Just a few more tugs.'

On the sixteenth tug, the portal widened slightly.

Erasimus shot through, rebounded off a mound of second-hand dentures, and plummeted into a pile of several billion used handkerchiefs.

He struggled to the top, tore the socks from his beak and wrestled himself free from the multitude of hankies and false teeth that clung to him. 'Gahhh!' he gasped. 'This has to be the least hygienic rescue I've ever had the displeasure of being involved with!'

'Could've been worse,' Jellybean said, motioning to the portal. Without the stork's body plugging the gap, it had already shrunk to the size of a pinhead.

With a soft '*Plip!*' it vanished.

Almost immediately, Jellybean went back to poking his bellybutton.

'Click! Click! Click! Click! Clickety! Clickety! Click!'

'Stop picking at it!' Erasimus snapped. 'It'll never recharge if you keep picking at it.'

Jellybean kicked a sock, launching it over the edge. 'But this place is rubbish.'

They watched the mist sink low over the landscape, revealing heaps of stamps, bus passes, pocket watches, diaries and concert tickets.

'Well, can't stand around all day.' Erasimus flexed his wings. 'I'll go scout out the lie of the land. You settle down and try to get some kip.'

'You want me to sleep here?' Jellybean said, wrinkling his nose. 'In all these socks?'

'Don't see why not. You've slept in worse places before; a demon's stomach, for one thing.'

'At least that had a bed in it.' Jellybean approached the edge and peered over. 'I could probably climb down. It's not that steep.'

Erasimus shook his head. 'Too risky. Could be miles to the bottom. You might slip and fall, and then where would you be?'

'At the bottom,' Jellybean said.

'Yes, but probably not in the best of shape, eh?'

'I bounced the last time.'

'That was just a one off,' Erasimus snapped. 'Inflatable planets don't grow on trees, you know.'

'Neither do shoes, usually,' Jellybean countered.

'No, you'll be much safer staying put. Who knows what horrors might lie waiting in the mist? Now lie back, close your eyes, and don't let the Laundry Monsters steal your socks.' Erasimus took to the skies and soared off.

'Laundry Monsters?' Jellybean said, glancing warily down at his feet.

'Oh, he's probably just pulling your leg,' rumbled a guttural voice from somewhere deep within the sock pile.

Suddenly the heap erupted, spewing socks in every direction. An enormous pair of bandaged hands reached upwards, gripped Jellybean tightly by the ankles, and dragged him screaming into the darkness.

'Wehey!' yelled Caspian. 'Three kings!'

Kings Creophageous, Ramekin and Hufty peered out at Caspian from behind their cards. 'What of it?' they said, as one.

'No, I mean I've got three kings.' Caspian spread his cards out on the dining table. 'It's an unbeatable hand.'

A huge gauntlet-clad fist smashed down on the table, upturning Caspian's goblet of wine. 'So's this,' King Creophageous rumbled. 'It's fought in many battles. Exploded many skulls.'

Caspian sighed. 'You're missing the point. I'm *winning.* You owe me money.'

The three royal opponents motioned to their attendants. Sacks of precious gemstones rained down upon the table.

'That seems to be happening rather a lot,' observed King Ramekin, as Caspian shovelled handful after handful of gemstones into his bottomless pockets. 'I'm not sure I like this "cards" thing at all.'

'Just a friendly game, you said,' grumbled King Hufty. 'I don't see what's so friendly about robbing us blind.'

'This is just the warm-up, mate.'

'We only stopped by to pay our respects before your coronation tomorrow,' King Creophageous rumbled.

'I only stopped by to borrow a cup of sugar,' said King Hufty.

'Perhaps it would help if I explained the rules again?' suggested Caspian.

'Just once would be a start,' said King Creophageous, in tones as icy as an arctic plain.

'The game's called Riches to Rags, right? The main aim's to build up your royal arsenal and avoid the beggar of the pack, or it's game over for you.'

King Creophageous leant across the table, and gazed down at Caspian's cards through the eye slits in his helmet. 'That king looks suspiciously like a beggar to me.'

'Yeah,' said King Ramekin, craning forward. 'Which someone's drawn a crown on.'

Caspian slipped his marker pen back into his pocket, and smiled innocently. 'A perfectly legal move. It's all in the rules.'

'In that case,' King Creophageous said, as he scrawled on his cards with a skull-tipped pen, 'I also have three kings.'

'As do I,' grinned King Ramekin, scribbling away.

King Hufty patted the pockets of his silk tunic, and looked from one king to the other. 'Er,' he said, 'does anyone have a pen I could borrow?'

'Tell you what – let's start a new game,' said Caspian. 'Are any of you fellows familiar with poker?'

The three kings exchanged puzzled glances.

'You mean the big hot pointy thing that goes up a peasant?' volunteered King Ramekin.

'Not quite. Still, I'm sure you'll pick it up as we go along.'

'That's what you said the last time,' King Hufty grumbled.

King Creophageous drained his last dregs of wine, and crushed the empty goblet in his fist. 'More!'

'Clarence!' Caspian hollered. 'Crack open another casket of Bladdered Wizard will you matey?'

'It's actually called "Wizard's Bladder", sire,' said Clarence, popping his head round the doorway. 'For reasons probably best left unmentioned. Am I to take it you'll be staying a while longer?'

'Looks like it.' Caspian retrieved the portal tracker from a puddle of wine, and rattled it next to his ear. 'This thing hasn't gone off in ages.'

'Perhaps it's broken, sire?'

'Nah, they're built to withstand abuse.' Caspian rapped the portal tracker vigorously against the table. 'More likely my friends have settled down for the night.'

'Maybe you should do the same, sire?' Clarence urged.

'Nonsense. The night is young, the cards are willing and the opponents reckless. Pour away, my good man. Pour away!'

'Aha! I've got a three, a seven and an instructions card,' said King Hufty triumphantly. 'That's good, yes?'

'Oh yes,' said Caspian, stretching his poker face to its limits. 'Very good indeed.'

13

The Fabled Lost City Of Spang

Erasimus returned to the sock heap several hours later to discover the top of the heap deserted, and Jellybean sat bare-foot at the bottom, doing a jigsaw with a twelve-foot tall mummy. Brian was graciously assisting, by eating all the green pieces.

'I gave you one simple piece of advice to follow...' Erasimus sighed, staring pointedly at Jellybean's feet.

'Shhh!' said Jellybean, eyes fixed firmly on the puzzle. 'Doing a jigsaw.'

'I can see that,' Erasimus said, eyeing the unwholesome creature sat opposite him. 'But who's she?' The mummy was wrapped from head to foot in multi-coloured socks, and smelt worse than Death's armpits after a hard day's reap.

'Laundry Monster,' said Jellybean.

'And where, pray tell, are your socks?'

'Dunno. Lost 'em.'

'Hurrah!' cried the Laundry Monster, jamming a piece of puzzle into place. 'Another bit of sky!'

'Ah, bravo! Bravo!' Erasimus let the false smile slide off his beak and whispered in Jellybean's ear. 'Might I have a word in private, please?'

'When we've finished the jigsaw,' Jellybean said testily.

'Finished it?' Erasimus ran his eyes up the enormous mountain of puzzle pieces. 'There must be at least ten billion pieces there.'

'Twelve billion, six hundred thousand, four hundred and thirty-two,' said the Laundry Monster, tongue dangling from the corner of her mouth, like a particularly soggy roll of red carpet.

'I see. Been at it a while, have you?'

''S right.' The Laundry Monster nodded. 'Us Laundry Monsters are very keen jigsaw enthusiasts. Everyone knows that.'

Erasimus inspected the puzzle and clucked with disapproval. 'Well you're not doing a very good job. You've got a bit of grass in the sky, for starters.'

'Me-e-e-eh!' said Brian, making a beeline for it.

'This ain't easy you know,' the Laundry Monster grumbled. ''Specially since each piece is from a completely different jigsaw.'

Jellybean frowned intently at the mishmash of jigsaw pieces they'd been forcing higgledy-piggledy on top of one another. 'You mean we'll never actually finish it?'

The Laundry Monster steepled her bandaged fingers together, and smiled. 'Look on it as the ultimate challenge,' she said. 'A test o' payshernce… the bonsai tree of jigsaw puzzles, if you will.'

'I give up,' said Jellybean.

'Ah, please yerself,' said The Laundry Monster. 'Fancy helpin' me pair these odd socks then?'

Jellybean yawned and stretched. 'Probably ought to be getting along, actually.' He turned to Erasimus. 'Did you find us somewhere to stay?'

'No, worse luck. There's nothing out there but endless heaps of garbage.'

'It's not garbage, it's lost property,' said the Laundry Monster. 'That's why there's so many flippin' teaspoons. Land of the lost, innit?'

Jellybean's stomach let out a rumble of distress. 'But I haven't eaten since the carnival.'

The Laundry Monster thrust her fingers between her bandages, and drew out a limp sandwich. ''Ere, slap your lips around that.'

Brian sniffed it, and turned up his nose.

'I'm not eating anything Brian won't touch,' said Jellybean.

Erasimus eyed the sandwich with caution. 'I suppose it's too much to hope that the stuff oozing out the side's cheese and pickle?'

'Sock-mulch and bunions, actually,' said the Laundry Monster, waggling her massive carbuncled toes at them. 'Made 'em meself, with me own fair feet.'

Jellybean and Erasimus exchanged glances.

'Come to think of it,' Erasimus said, after the briefest of pauses, 'I believe I did catch sight of a city on my travels. Just over there somewhere.' He gestured vaguely in the direction of a distant mound.

'We'll make for that then.' Jellybean yanked two stripy odd socks off the Laundry Monster's arm, and slipped them on.

'Oi! Cheeky rascal! Those are mine!'

'Not anymore,' Jellybean said, sliding his shoes over them.

'You'll be back!' the Laundry Monster hollered as they dashed off. 'There's only one city round 'ere, and you'd have to be *really* lost to find that place.'

'We are really lost,' Jellybean yelled back. 'We're not even on the right planet.'

Just to be on the safe side, they closed their eyes, span round a good dozen times, and struck off together in a random direction. Five minutes later, they were hopelessly and utterly lost.

'Welcome,' wheezed a cracked, gravelly voice, almost at once, 'to the fabled Lost City Of Spang!'

Jellybean risked a peek.

A blind old goblin was hobbling out from the city gates, pushing a shopping trolley that was stacked to the brim with an assortment of dusty old trinkets, baubles, knick-knacks and bric-a-brac. She stopped before them, and inhaled deeply through her impressively large nose. 'Let's see what we have here…' Her nostrils fluttered keenly in Jellybean's direction.

'Ooh, a cheeky little number!' she declared. 'A headstrong, weak bodied, full-blooded aroma with a certain rustic charm.' *Sniff! Sniff!* 'I'm gettin' burnt tyres…buckteeth…rotting apples…compost…yes, a definite eleven-fingered, banjo strummin' sorta texture, all topped off with a zesty, starlight tang.' She took a step back, and gave Jellybean one last sniff of appraisal. 'You must be Jellybean Snot Nose Stink Face Gator Bait You There Not Shawney Other One Skratcher.'

'Among other things, yeah,' said Jellybean.

'Then I believe these are yours.' She scrabbled around in the shopping trolley, and handed Jellybean a large plastic bag overflowing with teaspoons, odd socks, loose change, marbles, crayons, buttons, pipe cleaners, pencils, elastic bands, sweet wrappers, crisp packets and toenail clippings.

'What's all this?' he asked.

'Everythin' you've ever lost in yer life. Minus my finder's fee, of course.'

As Jellybean rummaged through the bag, he was surprised to discover all of the items had been individually labelled with the various names he'd borne over the years, along with where he'd been when he'd had the items last.

'Right, who's next?'

Before Erasimus could flap out of the way, the decrepit goblin's nose homed in on him. Her mighty nostrils quivered with excitement. 'Ah, now this one's much more complex…a heady bouquet of aromas, like a fine old wine.' *Sniff! Snfft!* 'An extremely old wine.' Her face soured, and her nose deflated. 'Well past its sell-by-date, if you want my opinion. Yes, I'm definitely detecting a stuffy, ancient odour about this one.'

'Steady on, old girl,' muttered Erasimus.

'And feathers…' continued the goblin, sniffing away. 'Not many feathers, granted, but certainly more than a dozen.'

'Now look here!'

Before Erasimus could finish his sentence, a tiny paper bag was thrust in his direction.

'Erasimus Terrence Rigwiddle, these, I believe, are yours.'

'It's Theodore,' grumbled Erasimus. 'The "T" stands for Theodore.' He opened the bag and squinted inside. 'Three paper clips? That's it, is it? That's the grand total of everything I've lost in my entire life?'

'It's yer own darned fault for bein' so careful where you put things,' said the goblin, waggling a finger sternly. She took a step towards Brian. 'And last but not least, we have –'

Her nostrils puckered. After a coughing fit that lasted several minutes, she said in a breathless, wheezing voice: 'Some sort of mobile sewage system?'

'We call him "Brian",' said Jellybean cheerily.

'And they call me Grandma Puddle,' said the goblin, stooping down to hand Brian half a lost boot. 'On account of me leaky brain, see?' She rapped her knuckles against a metal funnel sat on top of her head, and gave them a toothy grin.

'Oh my, that is quite something isn't it?' said Erasimus. 'Anyway, if you'd be so kind as to give us directions to a restaurant or something, we'll get out of your hair. Or funnel, as the case may be.'

'First,' Grandma Puddle declared, thrusting a walking stick dramatically into the air. 'We must consult the mystic runes!'

'Isn't there perhaps a guidebook or something?' Erasimus grumbled.

Grandma Puddle raised a commanding finger for silence. When she was sure she had their full atten-tion, she rummaged around in a tatty weather-beaten satchel and withdrew a scratchcard. Carefully she scraped away at the tiny silver panels with a gnarled fingernail.

Once the panels were uncovered, she brought the card close to her lips, thrust out a withered grey tongue and proceeded to systematically lick them.

Her expression soured.

'Three lemons,' she said gravely. 'This is a very bad omen!'

'No it isn't,' said Jellybean, craning over her shoulder. 'You've just won twenty dollars, look.'

Grandma Puddle nudged him in the ear with a bony elbow. 'The runes have spoken! They never lie!'

'Did these runes by any chance mention anything about a hotel?' said Erasimus wearily.

'No, but they did inform me you are about to embark upon a long, perilous journey from which there'll be no return.' Grandma Puddle span round and pointed a wavering finger at Brian. '*No return!*'

'We're already on one of those, actually,' said Jellybean.

'Yes, and we're all rather famished,' said Erasimus, 'so if you don't mind –'

'Well this particular journey's going to be even longer and with even *more* perils, all right?' Grandma Puddle snapped. She straightened her dripping funnel, gritted her teeth and continued. 'So it's just as well that the runes have decreed you'll have a highly respected guide to keep you out of harm's way.'

'Ah yes,' Erasimus beamed. 'That'd be young Jellybean here.'

'I'm a Navigator,' said Jellybean proudly.

Grandma Puddle scowled so hard that a jet of grey liquid squirted out the top of her head. 'They meant me! The runes meant *me!*'

'Did they ask for you specifically?' said Erasimus.

'Well no, but –'

'Then we'll bid you good day.'

They waded through Grandma Puddle's ever increasing puddle, and headed in through the gate.

Erasimus chuckled softly to himself. 'A blind tour guide! She must think we were born yester–' As his eyes fell upon the city, his sentence trailed off.

Everyone inside was wearing blindfolds, even the guards. Pedestrians stumbled this way and that, somehow managing to avoid one another and every-thing else in their path.

Much like the jigsaw puzzle Jellybean had attempted earlier, the city was full of missing pieces, and parts that didn't fit; there were stairs that led nowhere, streets that led everywhere except where people were trying to get to, upside down houses with upside down families living inside them, and shops without windows, doors and, in some cases, bricks.

'Right then,' said Jellybean, rooted to the spot.

'Right then,' said Erasimus.

'Meeeeeeh!' whimpered Brian.

A cart loaded with blindfolded sightseers rum-bled past, with blind horses and a headless driver at the helm.

'Perhaps now would be a good time for me to mention my rates?' said Grandma Puddle, as she shuffled in behind them.

The three companions stumbled off through the city, with their new guide pointing out various sounds, smells and tastes of interest along the route.

'And that,' Grandma Puddle said, shuffling to a halt, 'is the unmistakable sound of a Quasi-Cranial Kendo Mathematics tournament in progress.'

Jellybean strained his ears and listened, but all he could hear were the stork's leathery lungs rasping away beside him.

'For those not in the know, that's the lost art of attempting to recite complex mathematical equations, whilst an opponent beats you over the head with a big stick.'

Jellybean's fingers absently strayed to his blindfold. 'My Pa would've been great at that. 'Xcept for the maths bit.'

'No peekin'!' snapped Grandma Puddle. 'And you, quit tryin' to eat yours!'

'Meeeeh…'

'I really don't see what all the fuss is about,' said Erasimus. 'If they want to look, let them look.'

'Please yerself. But don't blame me if yer brain starts dribblin' out yer ears and yer eyes shrivel up like salted slugs.'

Jellybean instantly stopped fumbling, and let his hands drop to his sides.

'Very wise. Most sights in this city are best left unseen.'

They stumbled onwards a few paces.

'Now, if you thrust out yer tongue and waggle it around, you should be able to taste the unmistakable flavour of Grunk.'

'What's Grunk?' asked Jellybean, poking out his tongue.

'That crunchy yeller stuff that forms in the corner of yer eyes after a hard night's sleep,' said Grandma Puddle knowledgeably.

Jellybean hurriedly shut his mouth again.

'Judgin' by the taste of it, I'd say we're approachin' a Cyclops Grunk factory.'

'There's a market for that sort of stuff, is there?' said Erasimus doubtfully.

'Oh yeah, the leprechauns can't get enough of it.'

'Why?' asked Jellybean. 'What do they use it for?'

'To bury in pots at the ends of rainbows, and infuriate treasure hunters, of course. And we're walkin', we're staggerin', we're bumpin' inter stuff.'

They stumbled blindly onwards for what felt to Jellybean's empty stomach like an eternity, until the procession halted once more, and Grandma Puddle commanded: 'Blindfold's off! We're here.'

Jellybean tore off the blindfold, and found himself staring at the crooked paint-chipped door of a toilet cubicle. 'Here's not very impressive,' he concluded.

'Ah, you say that now,' Grandma Puddle beamed, 'but wait 'til you see what's inside!'

14

Sprout Cheese At The Thirteen Bells

What awaited Jellybean inside was far worse than a public toilet; it was a restaurant run by hunchbacks.

Glistening pink humps poked up through specially carved holes in the tables, their tops flipped open to reveal the diners' meals of choice (or, as the waiters attached to the serving humps preferred to put it, their chosen method of execution).

Several fully functioning toilets had been delicately arranged around the tables, to act as seating.

From the rafters dangled thirteen ornately carved bells, from which this particular restaurant took its name, clanging noisily away as hunchback waiters swung past overhead, dispensing beverages and condiments from their humps with an alarming lack of accuracy.

In a misguided attempt at adding a touch of class to the joint, lost classical paintings of various ugly characters lined the walls, all mounted at crooked angles. Jellybean found himself staring at one of Picasso's missing masterpieces, from his 'Wonky-eyed Wench' range. The woman in the picture had the sort of misaligned features only a hunchback could love.

'I say!' Erasimus hollered, attempting to pitch his voice over all the bell clanging and toilet flushing. 'More mashed earwig over here, if you'd be so kind!'

A hunchback who was attempting to evolve ugliness to brave new heights by adding a hair-lip and mono-brow into the mix, descended on their table. With cultivated disregard for social grace, he flopped open his hump, and ladled fat, wriggling earwigs over Erasimus' dinner.

'You're a marvel, dear sir!' Erasimus enthused. 'A marvel!'

'You want thome too, thort thtuff?' lisped the waiter, advancing on Jellybean's meal.

'I'm fine, thanks,' said Jellybean, shielding his food with his hands.

As Erasimus hoovered around inside a serving hump with the tip of his beak, crunching, slurping, slobbering noises filled the air. 'Oh, you don't know what you're missing.'

'If you've room for more,' Jellybean said grimly, 'you're welcome to the rest of mine.'

Erasimus squinted across at the half-eaten yellowy-green mass that sat wobbling away on Jellybean's dish. 'Why? What's wrong with it?'

'It's a bit…splook.'

'Nonsense! It'll put hairs on your chest.'

'And on my tongue.'

'Green stuff's good for you. Well known fact.'

'Yes,' said Jellybean slowly, 'but cheese fondue is supposed to be yellow.'

'Thorry about that,' said a voice from under Jellybean's side of the table. 'I had raw thprouth for lunch. They mutht've got mixthed in.'

Jellybean pushed himself back from the table, and folded his arms. 'I'm not eating hunchback sprout cheese.'

'Look on it as an adventure,' beamed Erasimus.

'Or a thuithide mithion,' said the voice from beneath.

Erasimus lifted the tablecloth, and frowned at the hunchback acting as Jellybean's serving dish. 'Will you kindly stay out of this, old sausage?'

'Thorry,' the hunchback grumbled. 'Jutht trying to take an interetht.'

'Let's try a different cubicle,' Jellybean urged. 'There might be a steakhouse next door.'

'I somehow doubt it,' Erasimus said, lowering the tablecloth. 'Only a hunchback would take such desperate and dastardly measures as to squeeze an entire restaurant into a toilet cubicle. Everyone's got to go sooner or later – and that's when they pounce!'

Jellybean's eyes momentarily followed Brian as he roamed from table to table, scrounging scraps from grateful customers. On several occasions, they attempted to give him a tip. 'Still, there's got to be better places to eat at than this.'

'It's not that bad.' Erasimus dipped his beak into the serving hump. 'These worms in tomato sauce are particularly appetising. I could eat them all day, and still have room for more.'

'That'th tapewormth for you,' sniggered a voice from under the table.

Erasimus squinted down at the long noodle-like object wriggling around in his beak. 'Tapeworms?'

With a shudder, he let it drop back into the hump.

'They've got ath much right to eat here ath any-one elthe, you know,' said the hunchback critically.

Erasimus gave an indignant cluck and hopped to his feet. 'Not if it's me they're eating. I'm not on the menu!'

'Come on, Brian,' Jellybean called. 'Looks like we're off.'

A snooty waiter with a nose so upturned it was practically touching his forehead lurched across the room towards them. 'Leaving already, thir?'

'No time like the present,' said Erasimus, attempting to duck past him. 'And presently, we'd rather be anywhere but here.'

'Very good, thir,' said the waiter, nimbly block-ing his escape route. 'And how will thir be paying?'

'With extreme reluctance, I should think.'

'Thocks or thpoonth, thir?' insisted the waiter, drenching them in saliva.

'That crafty goblin took all our socks and spoons as payment for her services, before she left us to fend for ourselves.'

'How about these?' asked Jellybean, slamming a jar of lost toenail clippings down on the table.

'Ooh, that'll do nithely thir,' lisped the hunch-back. 'Very generouth indeed!'

'You get what you pay for, I suppose,' sighed Erasimus.

As they left the restaurant, stars hung in the night sky, shining down upon the massive queue of cross-legged pedestrians that stood jittering outside the toilet cubicle.

'I wouldn't go in there if I were you,' Erasimus warned. 'The facilities leave little to be desired.'

They turned down a side alley, and found Grandma Puddle sat on a tatty sofa, stuffing her grizzled chops with a sizzling seafood platter.

'Ah, there you are dearies!' She aimed a caviar-stained grin loosely in their direction. 'How was your meal?'

'Not as pleasant as yours, I'll warrant.' Erasimus eyed the platter with envy. 'Where did you get that?'

Grandma Puddle motioned with a well-gnawed lobster claw towards the bins stacked against the rear of the toilet cubicle. 'Hunchbacks are a bit backwards when it comes to knowing what to serve to their customers, and what to throw away,' she explained. 'That's why all their food tastes like garbage, see?'

'You could've told us,' scowled Jellybean.

'What, and let you hog all the Black Forest Gateau?'

'There's gateau?' Jellybean's stomach let out a growl.

'Not anymore. I was very thorough.' Grandma Puddle cast her empty food tray aside, and dabbed the corner of her mouth with a napkin. 'Well, I expect you boys'll be wantin' to settle down fer the evening, so allow me to show you to yer lodgings.'

She leant back on the sofa, spread out an arm and said: 'Tadaaaaa!'

'You can't be serious. You expect us to sleep on that mouldy moth-eaten thing?' Erasimus eyed it with disdain.

'And goat-eaten,' said Jellybean, as Brian got stuck in.

'If you think you can find a better sofa,' said Grandma Puddle, 'you're welcome to look elsewhere.'

'Indeed we will, my good goblin. Indeed we will.' Erasimus turned back towards the alleyway. 'Come on, Jellybean. Follow me!'

Before he could take a step forward, the run-down buildings on either side of the alleyway switched places, and stacked themselves on top of each other like a really world-class game of Jenga.

'Um…' said Jellybean, watching them wobble precariously.

Erasimus clucked nervously under his breath. 'Right,' he said, turning back towards Grandma Puddle, 'after further consideration, we've decided to stay put. It is just the one night, after all.'

'Very wise, Beaky,' said Grandma Puddle. 'Well, since you have no further need of my services I'll bid you good evening.' And with that, she slid backwards into the sofa's crease and vanished.

'Oh well,' said Erasimus, as he collapsed in an exhausted heap on the sofa, narrowly avoiding a wayward spring. 'I'm sure things will look better in the morning.'

15

A Rude Awakening

C aspian woke to the sight of two eager gnomes attempting to strap themselves to his feet.

'Heh. Brilliant dream,' he mumbled, and then went back to sleep.

Several hours later, he awoke again to find the gnomes were still there.

He began to suspect this wasn't a dream after all.

'Morning, sire,' squeaked the one on his left foot.

'Lovely day fer a stroll,' commented the one on the right, with a wink.

'Oh no,' Caspian groaned. 'Did Clarence put you up to this? I thought I made it perfectly clear that I'm not into gnome-related garments.'

'Give us a try sire, that's all we ask,' squeaked the first gnome. 'You'll find we're actually quite comfy.'

'Yeah, walk us in a bit. Do a little twirl,' encouraged the second gnome. 'You'll be the envy of the entire kingdom with Hangnail and Bunion on yer feet.'

'That's us,' said the first gnome excitedly.

'I'd rather avoid hangnails and bunions, if it's all the same to you. Besides, I've got my own stylish robe and snug-fitting shoes.'

Caspian glanced around the royal bedchambers, searching for the items in question. His eyes fell upon various gruesome furnishings; a unicorn-horn candelabra rested upon a stuffed halfling bed stand; dryadskin drapes covered the window, throwing sickening shapes and shadows onto the walls; a centaur-flank duvet had been cast aside on the floor, and a glazed ent wood wardrobe hung ajar to reveal all manner of unspeakable gnome-skin fashion accessories inside.

'I've got to get Clarence to do something about that décor,' he muttered.

'I know what you mean, sire,' one of the gnomes squeaked. 'Those outfits are *so* last season.'

'Not like these glorious new shoes of yours, eh sire?' added the other gnome.

'Look, I'm not interested.' Caspian attempted to reach over the blubbery pink mass that was his stomach, and unfasten the gnomes. 'You'll just have to save your skins for your own personal use.'

'What, you mean sittin' around on a toadstool all day, danglin' a fishing rod into a pond?' The gnome on the left foot scrunched up his face in distaste. 'What sort of a life is that for a growing gnome, eh?'

Caspian wrestled with the double-knotted lace the gnome had bound itself to his foot with. 'Better than being skinned alive and worn as a pair of pantaloons. Anyway, it sounds rather pleasant.'

'Pleasant?' the gnome named Hangnail screeched. 'It's a flippin' nightmare, mate.'

'Yeah,' agreed the gnome called Bunion. 'Have you ever seen a gnome actually catch a fish? Answer me that, eh?'

Caspian stopped struggling with the lace a moment. 'Well, no, now you come to mention it.'

'Exactly. Can't be done. Pointless flippin' existence, mate. At least King Numbles gave us a sense of purpose.'

'Maybe it's down to the bait you're using,' Caspian observed.

'Bait?' said Hangnail.

'Wassat then?' asked Bunion, scratching under his pointy red hat.

'Surely you don't just expect the fish to jump straight out of the water and onto an empty hook?' Caspian scoffed.

'Why not?' asked Hangnail. 'It's a nice hook.'

'Yeah,' said Bunion, 'shiny an' everything.'

'You need to give them an incentive. Stick a big, juicy worm on the end, or something.'

'Ha! That's where you're wrong!' Hangnail declared. 'Fish don't eat worms. If they did, we'd have seen 'em diggin' around in gardens.'

'Yeah, that's birds you're thinking of,' said Bunion smartly.

'Then perhaps you should go bird fishing.' The lace snapped, sending the first gnome thudding to the ground. Caspian pulled off the next lace, and kicked the second gnome across the room. 'Now go on, hop it before I throttle the pair of you.'

The gnomes scampered off, shouting abuse as they left.

'Gnome hater!'

'Good luck findin' yer shoes!'

Caspian descended the stairs barefoot, his robe covered in graffiti which had been scrawled using suspiciously small handwriting. 'Fat Head' and 'Stinky Feet' were two choice phrases the anonymous vandals had left.

He padded into the dining room, and breathed a sigh of relief. The portal tracker still lay on the table, where he'd left it the previous night. The gnomes may have taken his dignity, but they hadn't taken his escape route.

Snatching it up, he slumped onto his dining throne and let his girth spill out onto the table and several surrounding chairs.

'Heavy night, sire?' whispered a voice so chilling and otherworldly that for a moment Caspian thought the Shrieking Banshee soup was repeating on him again.

'Heavy morning,' he grunted back, resisting the urge to flee to his bedroom and cower beneath the duvet. He peered cautiously around. There was no one in sight.

'Think yourself lucky, sire,' said the voice grimly. 'At least you're not dead.'

The hairs on the back of Caspian's neck stood up, sending a Mexican wave of terror tingling down his spine. 'Was that a threat?' he enquired, in a voice that was slightly higher than he'd have liked.

'Not exactly, sire.' A decaying corpse in a tatty burial suit shuffled silently out from behind a curtain, and grinned at him in that spccial way that dead things do. 'More a sort of observation.'

'Dear god!' Caspian cried. 'Please don't tell me you're the cook. It'll put me right off my breakfast.'

'Alas, food holds little interest to me these days,' said the corpse woefully.

'Good thing too.' Caspian's eyes desperately searched for something else to stare at, and fell upon a rolled-up parchment clutched in the corpse's rotting fingers. 'So, it's an autograph you're after, is it?'

'In a manner of speaking, sire.'

He prised the parchment from the cadaver's rigor mortis grasp, unravelled it, and fished around in his pocket for a pen. 'Right, who do I make this out to?'

'Sour Grapes,' said the corpse. He waited a moment for Caspian to finish writing *'Get Well Soon'* and then added: 'Royal assassin, at your service.'

The pen juddered to a halt. 'I sincerely hope not,' Caspian said. '*Guards!*'

'But you've already signed your death warrant, sire.'

Caspian studied the text at the top of the page. '"I, Caspian Thrall, do hereby pledge the sum of 10,000 grubnuts to Sour Grapes Enterprises, for the attempted termination of I, Caspian Thrall."'

'Payable in advance,' said Sour Grapes, 'if you don't mind.'

Caspian crumpled the parchment and tossed it over his shoulder. 'Take a hike, dead beat.'

'I assure you, I come very highly recommended. King Numbles used to swear by my services.'

'I bet he did. I'm sure I'd have a few nasty words to say if someone stuck an arrow in me.'

'Oh, I wouldn't be sticking them in you, sire, dear me no.' Sour Grapes shook his head, liberating a few maggots. 'Very bad for business, that sort of thing. Can't get repeat fees if I go round killing my employers. No, my field of expertise lies in near misses.'

'In that case I'm definitely not hiring you,' said Caspian, motioning to the door. 'The Caspian Thrall administration hires none but the best.'

'Please yourself, sire. It's your funeral.'

As Sour Grapes shuffled sombrely out, Clarence clattered in.

'Good morning, sire,' he chimed, laying a fully laden breakfast tray down on the table. 'Big day today.'

'Is it?' Caspian grunted. 'Well, good for you.'

'Even better for you,' Clarence beamed, 'what with your coronation and everything.'

'Yes, well let's not be too optimistic eh?' Caspian glanced at his portal tracker and gave it a meaningful tap.

'Even so, I've taken the liberty of preparing a little speech.'

'Breakfast first, speech later.' Caspian knocked back a cup of coffee, and gestured for a refill.

'Very good, sire.' Clarence reached for the coffee pot. 'And how are your new shoes treating you? Nice and snug, I'll warrant.'

'I'm not wearing any shoes,' said Caspian. 'You should've seen what those horrid little gnomes did inside them.'

A thin crease worked its way through the maze of worry lines that peppered Clarence's ample forehead. 'Not sure I follow you, sire. Shouldn't you be *wearing* the gnomes? They were made to measure.'

'Clarence, we spoke about this last night. As a general rule, I don't wear any item of clothing that might once in time have had a beard.'

'As it pleases you sire, though I expect the gnome union will have a thing or two to say about it. Now, would I be correct in assuming we have a rather special guest to add to this morning's festivities?'

'Eh?'

Clarence cast a sideways glance at the door. 'Our esteemed assassin in residence, sire.'

'Oh, don't worry about him,' said Caspian, waving a napkin dismissively. 'I told him to go bury himself.'

Clarence's trembling hands missed the mug, and splashed coffee over Caspian's cooked breakfast. 'Are you sure that was wise, sire?'

'I know you mean well, Clarence,' said Caspian, as he fished around on his plate and attempted to salvage a sausage, 'but I fail to see the point in paying good money to hire an assassin who can't even be bothered to do his job properly.'

'In that case sire, you'll be delighted to learn that Sour Grapes' assassination attempts tend to get a lot more accurate when his clients fail to make good on their payments.'

'Nonsense,' said Caspian. 'I've met his type before. All talk, and no trousers.' He mopped up the coffee spillage with a slice of fried bread, and shoved it into his mouth.

'Perhaps you'd care to examine those paintings behind you, sire?' Clarence gestured to a long line of paintings of unsavoury-looking kings from the kingdom's illustrious past. 'You might be interested to note their cause of death at the bottom there.'

Caspian ran his eyes along the paintings, and inspected the signature in their bottom left corners. He settled back in his seat, and took another swig of coffee.

'Probably just ate some bad fruit or something.'

'More likely they refused to hire a certain vengeful undead assassin. They don't call him "Sour Grapes" for nothing, you know.'

'You worry too much, Clarence. I'm a likeable sort of guy.' Caspian shot him a grin full of fried egg and sausage. 'Who'd want to kill me?'

The door flew open, and two guards raced in, puffing and wheezing. 'Enraged mob at the door to see you, sire,' said Lefty, with a hurried salute.

'Can't a man devour a sausage without the world caving in?' grumbled Caspian.

Outside, the sound of voices raised in protest grew in pitch. Somewhere close by, a window shattered.

'Did they, by any chance, say what they wanted?' asked Clarence.

'They were a bit shouty, but from what I could gather there's a rumour going around about the kingdom having gone bankrupt overnight.'

'That can't be right,' Clarence said. 'The kingdom's never been more prosperous. Why, we have a vast, sprawling treasury positively brimming with wealth.'

Caspian stared down at his plate, and studied his guilty reflection in the egg yolk. 'Ah, yes,' he said. 'About that...'

16

All That Glitters

Twin suns rose in perfect unison at both sides of the planet, catching the landscape in their glittering crossfire. Liquid gold lakes flared with a blinding intensity; gold dust beaches twinkled furiously.

Onwards the sunlight pushed through sparkling emerald hills and diamond-encrusted valleys, until finally it alighted upon the one object that even Mother Nature in all her glory couldn't possibly make glisten.

Jellybean sat up on the sofa, yawned, brushed off a couple of leprechauns who'd been attempting to mine Grunk from his eyes as he slept, and squinted around at his surroundings.

'Ugh,' he said.

He waited a moment for his eyes to adapt to the light, and tried again.

Around him, a garden full of sparkling flora twinkled away; gemstones the size of apples dangled enticingly above his head from the branches of golden trees. Delicate crystalline flowers blanketed the landscape. Solid gold statues of various heroic-looking figures peeked out from every nook and cranny.

Jellybean frowned at them in confusion.

Where was the alleyway from the previous evening? Where were the toilet cubicles that were chock-full of hunchbacks?

He looked around for his companions. They too were absent.

'*Briaaan!*' he hollered. '*Erasimuuuuus!*'

No bleat, no disapproving cluck. Nothing but his own voice, reverberating off a myriad of shiny objects.

Slowly it began to dawn on him that this wasn't the same planet he'd gone to sleep on. It wasn't even the same sofa; the previous one had been tatty and goat-eaten, whereas the one beneath him now was considerably more sparkly, adorned as it was with rubies, sapphires and a delicate gold trim.

He rested his chin in his grubby palms and thought back to the previous night. Memories began to bubble to the surface of his mind, like tiny morsels of meat floating in a giant brain casserole.

The alleyway had been cold and full of discomfort.

Springs from the sofa had dug into him from all angles, Erasimus' warbling snore had menaced his ears, and strange smells from the hunchback restaurant had hung in the air like thinly veiled death threats.

At some point in the night, a goat had attempted to eat his shoes, and then it had begun to rain. But not just any ordinary rain. No, it had begun to rain *spoons*.

Battered and bewildered, Jellybean had clawed his way into the thick crevice between the sofa's cushions, hoping to find shelter.

And then, suddenly, he was tumbling.

Down, down, down into the comforting darkness, where he'd lain amongst all the lost biros and empty crisp packets. Warm. Snug. Safe.

Sinking as he slept, until somehow he'd ended up here.

'Ugh!' said Erasimus, as he poked his head up through the sofa's cushions and grimaced at the scenery. 'I see you've discovered Teltamarok.'

'Yeah,' said Jellybean, shuffling over to let Erasimus squeeze past. 'It was down the back of the sofa.'

'The next time you decide to run off to a mythical golden planet in the middle of the night could you at least have the courtesy to let me know first?' Erasimus hopped up onto the arm of the sofa, and started irritably dislodging sweet wrappers and biscuit crumbs from his feathers. 'Gave me the fright of my life. For a moment, I thought you'd navigated without me.'

'It wasn't on purpose,' said Jellybean. 'I was trying to escape a downpour of lost spoons.'

'Ah, that explains why I awoke this morning with a teaspoon lodged in my ear,' mused Erasimus. 'For a few hideous moments I thought I'd been visited by the Earwax Fairy.' His eyes scanned the horizon. Several dragons wheeled by in the distance. Erasimus watched as they gracefully bobbed, weaved, and set fire to things. 'Marvellous beasts, marvellous!' he enthused. 'I do hope they don't devour us.'

Jellybean shielded his eyes and looked up at their vast scaly bodies. 'It's just a bunch of over-sized gators, flappin' around,' he shrugged.

'Dragons, my dear child. Dragons! It's all that gold, you see? They're drawn to it like…like…'

'Flies to a donkey's bottom?' suggested Jellybean.

Erasimus glared at him. 'You really know how to sap the magic out of things. Come on, let's go find that blessed goat of yours.'

'Isn't he back through the sofa?'

'No, I caught sight of his rear-end disappearing into it during the night. Thought it was all part of a rather extravagant dream, until I heard your voice hollering from within.'

'Probably went in search of me,' said Jellybean.

'More likely, he went in search of breakfast. Even Brian wouldn't chance eating at a hunchback restaurant twice.'

Their eyes locked as a troubling thought occurred to them.

'Let's hope we find him before he eats something expensive!' Erasimus blurted. 'The dragons won't take kindly to someone nibbling at their hoard.'

They hopped off the sofa and headed across the shimmering wilderness.

'Hey, maybe we should get Caspian a souvenir whilst we're here?' Jellybean scooped up a handful of gold nuggets from one of the many large mounds that littered the landscape. They were lighter than they looked, and warm to the touch. 'He'd always wanted to go to Teltamarok.'

'A lovely gesture,' said Erasimus, 'though dragon's dung is rarely considered the gentleman's gift of choice.'

Jellybean stared at the nuggets a moment, and then slipped them into his pocket with a grin. 'I won't tell him, if you don't.'

'Oh, and whatever you do, don't pick the little yellow flowers.'

'Flowers are fer stompin' on, not pickin',' said Jellybean, spieling off more words of wisdom from his dear deluded Pa.

'Best that you don't,' Erasimus cautioned, as Jellybean angled his boot towards the nearest clump. 'Those are Midas flowers, my dear boy. The merest touch of their fair petals is enough to turn man or beast instantly to solid gold.' Erasimus stretched out a wing to indicate the countless gold statues of unwary treasure hunters scattered across the fields.

And then they heard it – a pathetic whimpering carried softly on the breeze.

'Meeeh…'

'Oh dear,' said Erasimus glumly. 'I wonder how many Brian ate?'

They found him several hundred metres away, staggering stiffly towards them through a field of headless flowers. There was pollen around his lips, and a golden glow about him that was far from healthy.

The hapless goat glanced up at Jellybean with a faint glimmer of hope in his brown eyes. 'Me-e-e–' he managed, before his jaw locked, and his legs seized up.

Jellybean dashed recklessly through the mine-field of deadly flowers, and flung his arms around Brian's 24-carat neck. 'Aw, no!' he sobbed. 'My goat's gone golden.'

'At least that'll keep him out of mischief for a while.' Erasimus fluttered down and perched on top of Brian's head. 'Right, off we go then.'

'We can't just leave him here!' Tears trickled down Jellybean's cheeks. Where they touched the Midas flowers, they instantly formed into tiny golden nuggets of sadness.

''Course not – he's coming with us. "Never leave a man behind", that's my motto.'

'You left Caspian behind,' said Jellybean, blowing his nose on his chequered sleeve.

'That doesn't count,' Erasimus snapped. 'It was before I had the motto.'

Bracing his shoulder against Brian's shiny golden rump, Jellybean heaved away.

Erasimus watched him struggle a moment, then spat on his wing tips and rubbed them together. 'You'll never get anywhere like that. Leave it to the professionals, dear boy.'

'Are you sure you can manage?' said Jellybean, wheezing away from the effort. 'He's quite heavy.'

Erasimus flicked his scarf over one shoulder, and puffed out his chest. 'You seem to be forgetting; I've carried a troll before. A golden goat should be a doddle by comparison. So crack open a portal, and let's get this golden Billy into the sky!'

17

The Crowning Of King Caspian

The atmosphere in the throne room was electric, though only in the sense that it was highly dangerous and extremely likely to get someone killed.

That someone in question strode down a carpet made from red-hatted gnomes, ducking rotten vegetables and blowing kisses at the raging mob.

'Thank you! Most generous, though alas I've already eaten.' Caspian paused a moment to give his unruly subjects the royal wave.

The vegetable throwing intensified, catching Clarence in the crossfire.

'Haven't these people ever heard of confetti?' Caspian hissed, as his aide stumbled under a relentless barrage of mouldy tomatoes.

'I suspect they may have been more inclined to use it,' growled Clarence, 'had you not lost the kingdom's wealth in a late night poker game.'

'I said I was sorry. Geez...' Caspian bobbed his head as a prize-winning cabbage sailed past. 'Oh well, at least they're not very good shots.'

'Yes,' said Clarence, wiping cabbage juice from his eye, 'lucky us.'

'And what's with all these gnomes?' Caspian lifted a foot to look down at the red-hatted rabble that lay beneath. 'I'm finding it very difficult to avoid treading on them.'

'I believe that's the whole point, sire. I warned you there would be consequences if you didn't wear the ceremonial footwear.'

'Doesn't it hurt them?' asked Caspian, as he stomped onwards down the thin aisle that led to the throne.

'I shouldn't think so, sire,' said Clarence. 'They're a very hardy breed.'

'Arrrgh!' 'Nyaaargh!' 'Aiiiee!' 'Eeeeek!' went the gnomes from underfoot.

'Then why do they keep making that god-awful racket?'

'Ancient gnomish greeting, sire,' said Clarence swiftly. 'It means "delighted to make your acquaintance."'

'And a hearty good "Nyaaargh!" to you too, my little fellows.' Caspian dismounted the shrieking carpet and squeezed himself onto the throne. It was made from the bones of the previous king's enemies. Judging by the size of it, he must've had quite a few; the back was so high that it almost touched the ceiling. Caspian promptly decided that what it lacked in comfort it certainly made up for in sheer stomach-churning terror.

'Any chance of a cushion?'

'You'll be needing this, sire,' said Clarence, handing him his speech.

Caspian slid the hefty tome under his buttocks and shifted around. 'Ah yes, much better.'

'I meant for addressing the crowd. I was up all night writing it, and I think you'll find there's some very salient points in there which could well turn the tide of this little misunderstanding in your–'

'You know what, Clarence? I think I'm probably just going to wing it.'

Clarence stared at him, dumbstruck and dripping with veg. 'Er, are you sure that's wise under the circumstances, sire?'

'It's all up here, Clarry old boy.' Caspian tapped his finger against a piece of tomato that was stuck to the side of his head. 'Trust me, I know how to work a crowd.' He reached into his robe pocket, pulled out a kazoo and blew a triumphant note.

The room fell silent, though mostly out of confusion.

'Right, now that I have your attention, I'd just like to start by saying –'

Sh-Thunnnnk!

An arrowhead buried itself in the back of the throne, inches from Caspian's face. He stared at it a moment, then turned his eyes on the audience.

'Oh come on! At least give me a chance to put the crown on first!'

A decaying hand rose from somewhere near the back of the crowd. 'I do apologise, sire,' said Sour Grapes. 'I was attempting to kill you and appear to have missed.'

'Well don't let it happen again.'

'Perish the thought, sire.' Sour Grapes adjusted his aim with the bow. 'Though I'm ashamed to admit, I will have to charge you for that one.'

'Hah! You'll be lucky,' said Lefty, from where he sat at his hastily erected rotting vegetable stall. 'He ain't got no money.'

'Yeah, lost it all in a poker game,' said Righty, as he worked his way through the crowd, distributing vegetables from a large sack. 'Couldn't even afford to pay his most loyal guards. Tuppence a tomato! Come an' get h'your rotting tomatoes!'

Suddenly the throne room's thick oak doors exploded inwards, and three angry-looking kings stormed in, marching with such ferocity that even the gnome carpet parted before them.

King Ramekin drew himself to a halt before Caspian's throne, and thrust out an accusing gauntlet-clad finger. 'That man,' he bellowed, 'is a cheat, and a liar!'

'Well yeah, we know that,' said a voice from the crowd. 'What's your point?'

Caspian attempted to recline nonchalantly on his throne, which proved tricky with bones sticking into him from all angles. 'All right, Rammers? Have you and your mates come by for a rematch?'

'We are here,' rumbled King Creophageous, 'for your head!'

King Hufty peered out from behind King Creophageous' muscular bulk. 'And that cup of sugar, if you've got it.'

'If this is to do with last night's card game –'

'You cheated!' squealed King Ramekin, his face turning bright red. 'Admit it!'

Caspian spread his hands out innocently. 'Of course I cheated. We all did. I just happened to be a lot better at cheating than everyone else.'

'I'm not sure I understand, sire,' whispered Clarence, leaning in close. 'I thought you told me you'd lost?'

'Yeah, I may have lied a bit.' Caspian tapped the side of his nose and winked slyly. 'King's prerogative, eh?'

'Then what, may I ask, happened to all the wealth from the royal treasury?'

'It's in a safe place,' said Caspian, rapping out a merry little tune on his pockets.

A murmur of disapproval rippled out through an already pretty disapproving crowd.

'He's robbed the treasury,' grumbled one of the peasants. 'That's our taxes, that is.'

'It's not robbery if you're king,' declared Caspian loudly. 'Which I am.' He snatched the crown from Clarence's unresisting fingers and forced it down over his ears. 'Look, I've got dead fairies on my head and everything.'

'Not for long, matey boy!' rumbled King Creophageous, drawing his sword and stepping forward.

Before he could take a swing, Sour Grapes barred his path. 'If there's any killing to be done around here, I'm the man for the job.'

'Actually, I wouldn't mind having a go,' squeaked a little voice from somewhere low down in the audience.

'Me too.'

The two gnomes, Bunion and Hangnail, squeezed their way through to the front of the crowd.

'That man refused to wear us for this most joyous occasion.'

'He's a Gnomophobe!' cried Hangnail. 'A blatant Gnomophobe!'

Caspian looked around desperately for support, and found that even his trusty adviser had retreated to a safe distance.

'Off with his head! Off with his head! Off with his head!' chanted the crowd.

'Off with his toes! Off with his toes! Off with his toes!' countered the gnomes.

'Gentlemen, please…Leave it to the professionals,' insisted Sour Grapes, as he took careful aim with his bow.

'*Beeeeep! Target Locked!*'

With a sigh of relief, Caspian withdrew the portal tracker from his top pocket and jabbed its big green button. 'Aha!' he cried. 'Saved by the bellybutton.'

'*Destination accepted,*' declared the device. '*Portal piggy-back in ten seconds.*'

'Well, looks like it's time for me to stretch the ol' legs. Sort this lot out would you, Clarence?' Caspian had just enough time to Frisbee his crown in Clarence's direction, before his body was engulfed in a shimmering blue light.

'*Four…Three…*'

'…Two…One…Puuuuush!' cried Erasimus.

'I…am…pushing,' grunted Jellybean. Sweat glistened on his brow, his legs wobbled at the knees.

'Well flap your wings a bit.'

'I don't have any wings.'

Jellybean slumped to the floor, resting his back against Brian's smooth, golden body. In spite of their best efforts, he hadn't moved an inch.

Just a few short metres in front of them, the portal sparkled away.

Erasimus gave one last desperate flap, before he too collapsed in an exhausted heap.

'I thought you said you'd carried a troll before,' grumbled Jellybean.

'A baby troll,' wheezed Erasimus. 'More of a sort of large pebble, really. I suppose you'd best close that up whilst we rethink our strategy.'

'Hold on,' said Jellybean, squinting at the portal. 'I think something's coming through.'

Deep in its glimmering depths, a shape was beginning to form. Something large was working its way towards them. Something unsightly.

'Demons!' cried Erasimus.

Gradually, the shape took on features…a smug, circular face, a wide grinning mouth, twinkling mischievous eyes…

'That's no demon,' said Jellybean, as the figure drew closer. 'It's Caspian!'

Then, almost as suddenly as it had appeared, the grinning apparition vanished.

Something else emerged.

'I'm baaack!' yelled Caspian, as the blue glow faded.

Unwashed angry faces stared at him from all angles. Gnomes glared upwards, war-hungry kings frowned down, and everyone else seethed comfortably in the middle.

'Oh,' he said, realising that he wasn't quite where he'd expected to be. 'Er. Bear with me a moment.' His finger repeatedly prodded the portal tracker's big green button.

'Beep! Destination blocked!' trilled the portal tracker. *'Please consult tech support.'*

He continued hammering away at the button, until a thought suddenly occurred to him. 'Oh, right! The twenty-four-hour wizard replacement service.' Caspian shook his head, grinning like an idiot. 'Completely forgot about that...'

Sh-Thuuunk!

He blinked a few times, looked down at the shattered remains of the portal tracker cradled in his hands, and then at the long arrow shaft which had ploughed through it, into his chest. 'Ha!' he cried, pointing a victorious finger at Sour Grapes. 'You hit me! That saves a few quid.'

His eyes crossed, and he toppled to the ground, where he disappeared from sight beneath a swarm of angry gnomes.

18

Under New Management

'Do not be afraid!' bellowed Jellybean's brand new Techno Mage, as he stepped from the portal and spread his arms out wide. 'I am Balthazar Brittle, a mighty Techno Mage from the city of Chromebrood. And I –'

'You're not Caspian,' said Jellybean. He looked the stranger up and down. The new mage was older, taller, and considerably more bearded. He had scraggly white hair, a thick black robe and a nose so long and sharp it could've skewered a wild boar.

'No, I am Balthazar Brittle,' stated the mage, forcing a smile. 'And I am thrilled, nay delighted, that you have chosen one as humble as myself to protect you on your quest. Long have I prepared for this moment –'

'We're all right for Techno Mages thanks,' Erasimus interrupted. 'We've already got one.'

'Clearly you haven't,' said the mage testily, 'or I wouldn't be here would I?' He cleared his throat and continued in a booming voice. 'My heart is a glowing beacon of pride –'

'We left him behind on another planet,' said Jellybean.

'Not on purpose, mind,' added Erasimus. 'You see, there was this boulder that looked the absolute spitting image –'

'Well, his loss is most certainly your gain, my liege.' The mage pounded a frail fist on the ill-fitting body armour that glinted beneath his robe. 'My body is strong, my spirit is willing –'

'And your shoe smells vaguely of cowpat,' Jellybean finished for him. 'Yes, I know this bit.'

The mage's faltering smile flickered and died. 'Now look here, sonny,' he snarled. 'I didn't travel halfway across the universe to be verbally abused by some slack-jawed farmhand. Do you know who I am?'

'Balthazar Brittle?' intoned Erasimus.

'Aha, see!' The mage folded his arms smugly. 'Even your parrot has heard of me. My deeds are legendary.'

'Parrot?' Erasimus squawked. 'I'm a bally stork, you rotter!'

'You're a bird that talks, which makes you a parrot in my books. Now, will someone kindly close that portal before we catch our death of demons?'

'We're going through it in a minute anyway.'

'Too late,' said the mage, clutching his nose as a foul reek filled the air. 'Here they come!'

Something soft and squidgy slopped through the portal, and squelched at them.

'Ah, a Scotch Bloater,' said the mage, studying the pink gelatinous mass with a nostalgic look in his eyes. 'Been years since I've seen one of those. We used to use them as bagpipes, back in the day.' He drew back a foot, and booted the wailing creature back into the portal.

Jellybean hurriedly closed it up before any more unsightly hellborn things could squelch through and squidge at him.

'Now, let's talk business.' The mage rummaged in his pocket and pulled out a rolled-up parchment.

'What's that?' asked Jellybean, as the mage unrolled it.

'A contract, for services rendered. All you need do is sign on the dotted –' The mage's voice trailed off as he inspected the soggy white parchment in his hands. Grey lumps were hanging off of it. 'Ugh! What is this stuff?'

'Porridge,' said Erasimus. 'Caspian's doing, I'm afraid.'

'What sort of maniac puts porridge in his pockets?' tutted the mage.

'It wasn't deliberate,' said Jellybean. 'He was swimming around in it at the time.'

'The man sounds like a menace. I've a good mind to lodge a complaint!' Balthazar plunged his long, bony fingers into his pocket, and pulled out a piece of paper soggier than the last. 'Unbelievable! Even the complaints form has porridge on it. I know, I'll write "please see attached."' He scrawled angrily away with a pen, then paused a moment to give Jellybean an enquiring glance. 'What did you say his name was again?'

'Caspian,' said Jellybean. 'Caspian Thrall.'

'Never heard of him.'

'Are you sure about that?' said Erasimus. 'According to him, his deeds were also the stuff of legend.'

'Yeah,' said Jellybean, 'children sing songs about his exploits.'

'Well they don't where I'm from. I can assure you, I know every Techno Mage in the order, and there's not a single porridge-paddler among them.'

'So who the devil was he then?' asked Erasimus.

'Probably just some con merchant trying to work an angle.' Balthazar hovered impatiently over Jellybean's shoulder. 'Haven't you finished signing that contract yet?'

'I can't read it,' said Jellybean, squinting at the page. 'It's got porridge all over it.'

'Don't you worry about that,' the mage said. 'The details aren't important. It's the signature that counts.'

'Also, I can't write.'

The mage gritted his teeth, and tried his best to turn it into a grin. 'Just put an X.'

Jellybean looked to Erasimus for assistance.

'It's like a star shape, except with four points instead of five.'

Tongue hanging out in concentration, Jellybean proudly carved his first signature into a dry lump of porridge.

The mage snatched the contract back, rolled it up and slipped it into his pocket. 'Right, that's the first step over with. Let us now broach the matter of payment.'

'Payment?' Erasimus frowned. 'For what?'

'Saving you from that fearsome demon, of course. May it be the first valiant rescue of many.'

'Caspian never charged us for his services,' said Jellybean.

'Probably because he wasn't a proper Techno Mage,' said Balthazar. 'We don't come cheap, you know. There are all sorts of costs involved. You've got travel expenses, wear and tear on the robe, hazard pay, companionship fees…'

'In case you haven't noticed,' said Erasimus, spreading out a wing to indicate the glittering golden horizon, 'the whole planet's teeming with riches.'

'Oh no, don't try and palm off that cheap imitation tourist garbage on me. I wasn't born yesterday, you know.' Balthazar rapped his knuckles against Brian's golden bonce. 'I mean, what is this thing even supposed to be? A camel? A moose? It defies description.'

'That's Brian,' said Jellybean. 'And he's my goat.'

'Oh, I see. A family heirloom, is it? Has considerable emotional value, yes?' The mage beamed widely through his copious whiskers. 'Very well, I accept your tribute. Shake on it?'

Jellybean glowered at the mage's outstretched hand. 'No. He's mine.'

'On the other hand,' whispered Erasimus, 'if this imbecile is going to insist on accompanying us, we might as well let him do all the heavy lifting, what?'

'But –'

'We can't move him by ourselves. It's either that, or he stays here.'

'All right,' sighed Jellybean, reluctantly shaking the mage's clammy hand. 'It's a deal.'

'A very wise decision.' Balthazar Brittle cracked his knuckles noisily. 'Let's get this golden goat of mine airborne.'

'I've already tried that,' said Erasimus. 'He's too heavy.'

'Perhaps you weren't using the right tools for the task?' The mage rummaged around in a pocket, pulled out a collar full of tiny, flickering lights, and slipped it around Brian's neck.

'Why are you putting a collar on him?' scoffed Erasimus. 'It's not like he's going anywhere.'

'He will be in a minute.' Balthazar produced a remote control from his other pocket. 'Observe!' He pulled back on the remote's throttle, and Brian rocketed upwards like a goat-shaped model aeroplane.

'Aw, that's brilliant that is,' said Jellybean, watching his goat whiz back and forth. 'Can I have a go?'

Balthazar slapped away Jellybean's grasping fingers and moved the remote control out of range. 'Certainly not. Get your own flying goat.'

'Ah go on,' Jellybean pleaded, jumping up and down. 'Just one go.'

'Wheeeeeeeeeeeeeeeeeeee!' cried the mage, racing Brian through thc sky. 'Gosh, this really is a lot of fun isn't it? See that goat glide! I don't know about you, but I'm having a marvellous time!'

After forcing Jellybean to endure a full twenty minutes of astounding aerial goat displays, the mage finally brought Brian in to land. 'Right, enough merriment,' he declared. 'The tavern beckons. Navigator? Portal, if you please.'

'Do it yourself,' said Jellybean sulkily.

'Can't. Haven't got a magic bellybutton. Now be a good lad, and perhaps later on I'll give you a go on the goat. You'd like that, wouldn't you? Hmm?'

Jellybean shuffled his feet and grumbled. 'Aw, okay.'

A portal whummed open, looking considerably less shiny than usual against all the shimmering splendour that surrounded it.

Erasimus took a step towards it.

The mage instantly barred his path and thrust out the palm of his hand. 'Where do you think you're going?'

'With Jellybean, of course. The lad and me are inseparable. I'm taking him home to meet his parents.'

'Sorry,' said the mage firmly. 'No pets.'

A strangulated gurgling noise clawed its way up through Erasimus' gullet, and squeezed itself out through the tip of his stammering beak. 'Pets?' he screeched. 'The nerve! The cheek! I'll have you know I'm a stalwart companion. A bosom buddy!'

The mage raised a single bushy eyebrow. 'All right, what are your skills?'

'Eh?'

'Badger britches there opens portals to different planets, I smite demons with my amazing techno-wizardry. What do you bring to the team?'

'I'm a flyer!' barked Erasimus. 'And proud!'

'So's my goat,' said the mage, as he made Brian do another loop-de-loop. 'This means nothing to me.'

'And I, er, I also, uh –'

'He lays eggs,' cried Jellybean. 'Big ones!'

'I do what now?' screeched Erasimus.

Balthazar stroked his beard thoughtfully. 'Hmm…I must admit, I am quite partial to an egg sandwich. What quantity of eggs are we talking here?'

'Are you absolutely barking? I'm a *male* stork, you blithering –'

'One a day, every morning,' lied Jellybean. 'Regular as clockwork.'

'Well then Mr, er…'

'Erasimus T. Rigwiddle,' Erasimus hissed.

The mage's thick white eyebrows scrambled up his forehead, and took refuge in his hairline. 'Seriously?' he spluttered. 'Good god.' He composed himself, and continued. 'Well then, Mr Erasimus T. Rigwiddle…Egg-layer extraordinaire. Welcome to the team.' He slapped Erasimus on the back in a comradely fashion, strode up to the mouth of the portal, and turned. 'Oh, and I feel it's only fair to warn you that if you fail to deliver on my eggy morning repast, I'm also quite partial to a chicken dinner.'

Before the hideous gurgling noise in Erasimus' throat could form an appropriate response, the mage stepped through the portal, taking Brian with him.

'You know,' said Erasimus, once his eye had finished twitching, 'I do believe I'm actually starting to miss our old Techno Mage.'

19

Hard Porridge

In a deep, dank dungeon beneath the troubled kingdom of Muck, sat a particularly troubled wizard. His only company was the skeletal remains of an unsuccessful jester that dangled from a cage attached to the ceiling, and the rats and cockroaches that scurried across the cell floor.

On the wall opposite hung an empty set of manacles, hinting at a far from promising future.

Caspian surveyed his new kingdom, and found it wanting.

'Oh well,' he said, absently fondling the small hole in his armour where Sour Grapes' arrow had struck. 'Could be worse.'

A metal hatch in the top of the door slid open and Clarence peered in, a crown of golden fairies shimmering away on his head. 'Glad to hear you think so, Mr Thrall.'

'Ah, my trusty adviser Clarence,' intoned Caspian, as he rose to greet him. 'Come to return my crown?'

The corners of Clarence's thin lips curled up into a smile. 'I'm afraid the people have decreed that I hang onto it for a bit. And it's King Clarence now, if you don't mind.'

'Oh I see,' muttered Caspian. 'It's like that is it? After all I did for them.'

King Clarence tilted his head at an enquiring angle, making the crown slide around on his scalp like an ill-fitting wig. 'Such as..?'

'I killed their tyrant, and…and…slew all those dragons,' said Caspian.

'Dragons, Mr Thrall?'

Caspian waved a dismissive hand. 'I'm sure you've heard about them in the songs.'

'The only song *my* subjects are singing is "off with his head, off with his head!"'

'Are you absolutely sure they're not singing it about you?'

'Mr Thrall!' King Clarence barked. 'In the space of a single evening you stole all their wealth, bankrupted the kingdom, and brought us to the brink of war with our three most powerful neighbours.'

'It was my first day.'

'And unless you want this to be your last,' King Clarence snarled, 'you'll tell me where you hid all the loot.'

'All right,' said Caspian, folding his arms defiantly, 'what's in it for me?'

King Clarence's eyes narrowed to thin slits. 'The entire kingdom is out baying for your blood, and you're trying to cut a deal?'

'A knighthood, maybe,' mused Caspian. 'Or perhaps a statue built in my likeness, overlooking an orphanage or a nunnery.'

'Why don't you ask for a full pardon whilst you're at it?' sneered King Clarence.

'Well that goes without saying.' Caspian thrust his hands into the pockets of his robe, and rocked backwards on his heels. 'After all, I hold all the cards.' His smile froze. A small frown tugged at his portly features.

He pushed his hands further into the pockets, and fumbled around. Panic flashed across his eyes.

'I really don't have time for this,' snapped the newly anointed king. 'Thanks to you, I'm now a very busy –'

'Yes, yes, hold on a second,' said Caspian irritably, as he rummaged away. 'Can't you see I'm having pocket problems?'

Teeth gritted, grunting with effort, he forced both arms in up to the shoulders, and stretched his fingers out as far as they would go.

After several minutes of frantic scrabbling, he withdrew two empty hands.

'Unbelievable!' he cried, rolling his eyes at the ceiling. 'They've only gone and changed my pocket's frequency!'

King Clarence massaged his forehead with his few remaining fingertips. 'Where is the money, Mr Thrall?'

'I'm kind of wondering that myself,' murmured Caspian. Just to be sure, he took off his robe, turned it upside down and gave it a good shake.

On the seventh shake, an envelope fluttered out. It was addressed to Caspian in a large, important-looking typeface and bore the official seal of the Techno Mage order.

'Mail from your adoring fans?' enquired King Clarence.

'Somehow I doubt it.' Hands trembling, Caspian tore open the envelope and scanned its contents.

Dear Mr Thrall,

Due to crimes too numerous to mention, including cheating, lying, gambling, robe theft, impersonating a Techno Mage, and clogging a pocket portal with porridge, it brings me great delight to inform you that your services (whatever they might be) are no longer required.

All pocket privileges are hereby revoked, as is your right to exist on this or any other planet. Please terminate yourself immediately.

Wishing you a swift and unpleasant death,

Selina Skorn, High Commander of the Belly-button Brotherhood.

'Well?' asked King Clarence impatiently, as Caspian began to reread the letter. 'What does it say?'

Caspian carefully folded the letter in half, slipped it back into his pocket, and favoured King Clarence with a waxen grin. 'Is there any chance,' he said hoarsely, 'that I could have that pardon in advance?'

The metal hatch clanged shut, plunging him into darkness.

'I'm hungry,' said Jellybean, as they marched through the undergrowth of a drab and dreary planet.

'And I'm thirsty,' responded Balthazar Brittle. 'Five hours, forty seven planets, and not a single tavern in sight.'

'Yes, well, navigating's not a precise science, you know,' said Erasimus. 'There's all sorts of complex mathematical equations that need to be taken into consideration. Isn't that right, my dear boy?'

'Er, yeah,' said Jellybean. 'Sums and that.'

Balthazar stopped dead in his tracks, and span to face Jellybean. 'How many fingers am I holding up?'

Jellybean frowned in concentration at the Techno Mage's outstretched palm. 'Eleven?' he hazarded.

The mage inspected his hand quizzically. 'Eleven? Who in the world has eleven fingers?'

'My brother Shawney,' said Jellybean with pride.

'And did he, perchance, teach you how to count?' enquired the mage.

'Yeah,' said Jellybean, 'but I wasn't very good at it. I've only got ten fingers, see?'

'Aha!' cried Balthazar. 'It's as I suspected. This oily little brat doesn't know the first thing about navigating.'

'Jellybean!' Erasimus said in his most commanding voice. 'How many stars in the sky above?'

Jellybean glanced upwards, trying his best to ignore the golden goat soaring lazily overhead. His Navigator eyes pierced through the clouds and scanned the twinkling black heavens. 'Fifty one billion, six hundred thousand, eight hundred and thirty two,' he said automatically.

Balthazar looked to the sky, adjusted the setting on his glasses, and did a quick bit of mental arithmetic. 'Lucky guess,' he grumbled. 'And where's my eggs?' He shot an accusing glance at Erasimus. 'I distinctly recall being promised a big tasty egg every morning, regular as clockwork.'

'It's the middle of the afternoon.'

'On this planet, yes,' said Balthazar smartly. 'But it wasn't on those last twelve planets we passed through. I demand my dozen eggs!'

Erasimus shuffled his feet, and coughed. 'Yes, well egg laying's not a precise science either.'

'Yeah, there's all sorts of complex whatsits involved,' said Jellybean.

'A lady stork for starters,' said Erasimus under his breath.

'When I get hungry, I get cranky,' snapped Balthazar. 'And when I get cranky, flying golden goats tend to violently crash into things.'

To emphasise his point, Balthazar pulled back on the throttle of his remote control, and sent Brian's helpless golden body spiralling into a death dive. 'Oh dear!' he cried. 'Why, I do believe I'm encountering some turbulence!' Brian span recklessly through the air, skimming treetops and shaving branches. 'He's going down! Oh no!' Balthazar grimaced. 'He's probably going to hit that really big tree!' He turned to Jellybean, eyes wide in mock horror. 'I do hope his head doesn't come off…that would be *awful!*'

'All right, all right,' cried Jellybean. 'I'll take us to a tavern.'

'Oh, would you look at that?' said Balthazar, as he skilfully wove Brian around the tree and brought him in to land. 'I appear to have regained full control.' He glanced sideways at Erasimus. 'That's what comes from being a really *skilled* flyer.'

Jellybean closed his eyes, crossed his fingers, and plunged them into his bellybutton.

It was either good fortune or immense back luck that led them to step through a portal into the grubbiest tavern the universe had to offer. A large fireplace in the centre of the room pumped thick acrid smoke into the air, artfully concealing the dodgy dealings of the tavern's cutthroat clientele.

It was the type of place that could be said to have character; unfortunately it was the sort of character that would happily slide a knife between your ribs and steal your kidneys.

All eyes turned to the three newcomers, ending their travels on the large golden goat sparkling conspicuously at their side.

Meaningful looks were exchanged, and conspiratorial whispers filled the air.

'Ah! Just when I was starting to doubt your abilities, Navigator – you've finally done it,' declared Balthazar. 'A quaint, honest drinking establishment.' He pushed a dead body out of a chair, sat down, and snapped his fingers. 'Barmaid! A flagon of your finest ale. As you can see, money is no object.' He stretched out an arm to indicate Brian.

'Yes it is,' said the barmaid, scratching her tousled red hair. 'It's a goaty sort of object.'

'And it's all yours for the right amount of beer,' said Balthazar, with a wink. 'And perhaps a meal or three.'

'She's not having Brian,' growled Jellybean.

'Of course not.' Balthazar tapped his nose slyly. 'I have a plan.'

Their food arrived with a swiftness that could only be brought about by the presence of a solid gold goat. Although it wasn't the best meal Jellybean had ever tasted, after his recent encounter with hunchback cuisine, it certainly wasn't the worst.

He wolfed down a generous portion of Minotaur Medley, and helped Erasimus polish off the Mystery Fish supper.

Balthazar knocked back his fifth ale, licked the last few morsels from his plate, and belched loudly across the table. 'Better out than in,' he announced.

'Easy for you to say,' grumbled Erasimus, combing back his ruffled feathers. 'You weren't on the receiving end.'

Through the tavern's thick smoke, three shady figures approached. One was thin, with sly, weasely features. The two that flanked him on either side were impossibly wide, like a wall of tattooed flesh; what they lacked in necks they more than made up for in biceps.

The weasel-faced man leant on the back of Erasimus' chair, and treated Balthazar to a broken-toothed grin. 'Say…that's a nice goat.'

'Yes, she's a beauty all right,' said Balthazar.

'I'll give you two arms for it.'

'That's a tempting offer,' said Balthazar, 'but as you can see I've already got two arms.'

The weasel-faced man drew a thin blade, and leaned in close. 'You won't have,' he hissed, 'if you don't give me that goat.'

His two muscular companions lurched forwards, cracking their knuckles purposefully.

'Well that seems like a good deal,' said Balthazar, maintaining his cool, 'but here's what we'll do instead.' With casual ease, he slipped a metallic wand from his pocket, and pressed a button on its side.

A '*Click!*' a '*Hummm!*' a flash of green light, and then, where once three men had stood, there were now three sticky-looking puddles.

'Good gracious! Y-y-you killed them!' stammered Erasimus.

'No I didn't. I simply rearranged their molecules for a bit.' Balthazar pointed his wand at the bubbling mess. 'They'll be right as rain come morning.'

Jellybean watched with interest as a scruffy little dog trotted up to one of the puddles, sniffed it, and started lapping it up.

'How about now?' he asked.

'Well, all right, perhaps not now,' admitted Balthazar. 'But they've only got themselves to blame.'

''Ere, that's murder, that is,' said the barmaid, casting a critical eye over the scene.

Balthazar casually waved his wand in the barmaid's direction. 'Hm..?'

'Had it coming, mind,' said the barmaid swiftly. 'Well done you.'

'I think I've had all the food I can stomach,' said Erasimus, pushing his plate away.

'Nonsense! Somewhere in the universe, a curry house is calling.' Balthazar got unsteadily to his feet. 'Navigator, if you'd care to do the honours?'

A portal whummed open.

'Hey! Where do you think you're going?' cried the barmaid. 'You owe me for the meals.'

'Eh? Oh, right. Yes,' said Balthazar. 'If you could excuse us a moment, whilst I have a quick whip-round from the boys.'

'But the goat's right there,' said the barmaid, frowning.

Balthazar made shooing motions with his hands. 'Run along! Run along!'

'Okay,' whispered Jellybean, once the barmaid had backed off, 'what's your plan?'

Balthazar casually swung a leg over Brian's body, and eased himself down. 'Now we ride!' he yelled, kicking his heels into Brian's flank. 'Ride for the hills!' He pulled back on the throttle of his remote control, and with a hearty cry of 'yeeee-haaaaawww!!!' rocketed through the portal.

20

Bugs For Breakfast

Caspian sat on his cold stone bunk, picking cockroach out of his teeth.

It had been a good few years since he'd eaten bugs, and only then it had been as a dare, or a misguided attempt to impress girls.

Had he realised back then that they came in so many interesting flavours, he would have kept at it. Woodlice, for example, had an oaky sort of aftertaste, whereas stag beetles carried just the mildest hint of venison. As for dung beetles, well, best avoided altogether. He'd learnt that one the hard way.

Sure, it might just be the starvation talking, but he had to admit these last few weeks had certainly given him a taste for the crawlier things in life. He was becoming quite the beetle connoisseur. He longed for that satisfying crunch of teeth on shell, and that delightfully warm soft centre.

His ears pricked up.

Something in the corner of the cell had rustled.

He scrambled down from his bunk, and hauled his thin, pasty frame over to the mouse hole (anyone who said Caspian was half the man he used to be was being overgenerous. There was barely a quarter of him left).

The noise was coming from inside.

'Rats!'

A wide grin spread across his grime-encrusted features. So far, he hadn't managed to catch a rat. But today he was feeling lucky.

Boot off, heel at the ready, he crouched beside the mouse hole and waited.

'Hang in there, Alan,' he whispered, glancing up at the skeletal jester dangling above him. 'Supper is but a rat's whisker away.'

Movement. A sudden flash of silver as something raced through.

'Take that, you hairy nightmare!' Caspian yelled.

He brought the boot crashing down with every last pitiful ounce of strength…

And stopped, inches from his intended target.

For a moment he sat there in stunned silence, baffled by what had emerged.

It was a fish. And, what's more, it was waving at him.

'Hullo squire, it's me,' said the fish.

'But of course it is,' Caspian brayed. 'What a delight!' He could feel his sanity trickling out of his ears. His eyes strayed back to the mouse hole, idly wondering what would be next to emerge; perhaps a sombrero-clad aubergine playing the Maracas?

'Bunion,' said the fish.

Caspian blinked at it. 'You what now?'

'In case you don't recognise me.' The gnome peered out from beneath the large fish supported on his head, and beamed.

Caspian breathed a sigh of relief. 'I'm not going mad then?' His eyes scanned the cell floor. 'Where's the other one?'

'Inside the fish,' came a muffled voice.

'And why wouldn't you be?' said Caspian, grinning a little too widely.

'I was bein' bait, see?'

'So, now you're inside a halibut and seeking revenge, eh? Well go on, do your worst.' Caspian thrust a mucky foot in the gnome's direction. 'Remove an entire toenail if you have to. I don't care any more.'

'Actually, we wanted to thank you.'

'Yeah,' agreed the voice from inside the fish. 'You've given our lives purpose. We're the first gnomes in history to ever catch a fish. If there's ever anything we can do for you in return, just say the word.'

Caspian stared ravenously at their catch of the day. Drool trickled down his thick, matted beard. 'You could give me that fish, for starters.'

'I was going to mount it on the wall as a trophy,' grumbled Hangnail.

'Don't worry, Hangnail. I'm sure this is the first of many.' Bunion laid the fish before Caspian's feet, and bowed. 'The fish is yours.'

'Could you at least help me out of it first?' sulked Hangnail.

After a few squeezes of encouragement, the gnome popped out. Before he hit the ground, Caspian had already devoured the fish, bones and all.

'Suppose we'd best get back to our fishing, then.'

'My turn to be bait!' shrieked Bunion excitably.

Caspian settled back on his bunk, and smiled. 'Actually, before you go, there's one other teensy favour I'd like to ask…'

21

The Thingimagist

Jellybean leapt from the portal, and hit the ground running.

His feet churned up the soft earth of a lush green planet, untouched by civilisation until now.

THRUUUUUUM!

The ground shook as something landed heavily behind him.

He glanced back over his shoulder to see a huge, hairy shape lumbering towards him, drool dangling from its slavering black lips.

'It's still with us!' cried Erasimus, from somewhere above. 'Keep going!'

Balthazar swerved chaotically past on Brian's golden body, almost bowling Jellybean over. 'Bellybutton! Bellybutton! Bellybutton!' he commanded.

'I'm trying!' yelled Jellybean, finger poking frantically away.

'What we need is a garden gate,' stated Balthazar. 'That'd stop the beast in its tracks.'

Ahead, the faint outline of a portal appeared.

Erasimus swooped towards it. 'Don't wait for me. It's already fading!'

'Wasn't going to,' said Balthazar as he raced through.

A rock snagged the curly toe of Jellybean's shoe. He stumbled, skinned his knees, scrambled upright and forced himself onwards.

Hot, fetid animal breath steamed down the back of his neck. A deathly stench filled his nostrils.

The portal flickered once, twice…

I'm not going to make it, he thought. *I'm not –*

Then he was through, landing on the other side with a soft, wet splat. He rolled in the mud, and glanced upwards.

Inside the portal, a beastly shape was forming. It threw back its head, opened its cavernous mouth and –

Whumf! The portal vanished, leaving a blood-curdling howl echoing across the space between worlds.

Jellybean lay trembling in the mud.

'Well, that was a bit of a wheeze!' said Balthazar, as he dropped from the tree branches between which Brian's golden body was now firmly wedged. As soon as his feet hit the floor, foul reeking mud flowed into his boots and oozed between his toes.

A lumpy, bird-like shape dragged itself towards him from the clinging swampy mire. 'You had to do it, didn't you?' spluttered Erasimus. 'You had to go and tip a sleeping Minotaur!'

'I was just having a laugh,' said Balthazar, standing on one foot as he ejected a frog from his boot. 'Anyway, in some cultures running away from a giant angry bovine is considered a great test of courage. And I'm glad to say you both passed with flying colours.'

'I almost got a horn up the bottom,' said Jellybean miserably.

'But I bet it made a man of you, eh?' Balthazar ruffled Jellybean's muddy, sweat-drenched hair, and then wiped his hand on the back of his robe. 'Can't wait to see what adventures the next planet holds.'

Jellybean scrambled backwards in the mud, until his back was resting against a tree trunk. 'Need to recharge.'

'What, here?' Balthazar glanced around at festering swampland full of gnarled black trees and thick, choking vines.

'It's not so bad.' Jellybean sniffed the rancid air and let out a sigh. 'I used to live in a place like this.'

A vacuum cleaner on scaly alligator legs waddled past, sucking at flies with its hoover attachment.

'All right,' Jellybean admitted, as they watched it go, 'maybe not *exactly* like this.'

'Suppose I might as well get comfortable.' Balthazar thrust a hand in his pocket, pulled out a hammock and started setting it up. 'I trust you all brought hammocks? No? What a pity.'

Erasimus flapped awkwardly up, and alighted on a vine next to him. 'Before you get settled in, I believe now might be a good time for us to have a little chat.'

'Sorry. I do not converse with wildfowl,' said Balthazar, swatting irritably at him.

'Very well,' Erasimus scowled. 'I'll talk and you can listen. We've been travelling together for a month now –'

'Fun times,' sighed Balthazar. 'Happy memories!'

'For you, perhaps. For us, every day has been a nightmare, fraught with endless life-threatening situations.'

'Just as well I'm here to protect you then,' beamed Balthazar.

The scowl deepened. 'Situations that you put us in. You've already got us barred from eighteen planets.'

'You exaggerate.' Balthazar wound a rope from the hammock around a tree and fastened it off. 'It's sixteen at the most.'

'You appear to be forgetting those peace-loving centaurs we encountered several planets back. The ones who, within five seconds of meeting you, were threatening to ride us off a cliff.'

'All I said was "Horsey want a sugar lump?" Talk about overreaction.'

'The same might be said for you, when you encountered that unfortunate family of griffins.'

'Now that was basic self-defence. As any fool can tell you, one look from a griffin's eyes is enough to turn a man to solid stone.'

'That's gorgons, you imbecile,' glowered Erasimus, 'not griffins.'

'Is it?' Balthazar frowned. 'I always get those two mixed up. Oh well, no harm done.'

'You turned them into puddles!'

'I'm sure they'll get over it.'

'And must you always yell "witch" at every harmless old lady who crosses our path? It's most impolite!'

'I'll get it right one day.' Balthazar tapped his sizeable conk. 'Law of averages.'

'The point is, it's not the sort of behaviour that's becoming of a gentleman.'

'If you don't like it, get your own Navigator.' Balthazar swung himself up onto the hammock, closed his eyes and settled back. 'Though you might have a bit of a challenge finding one, since they're all dead.'

Erasimus' grip on the vine tightened, snapping it in two. He plunged headfirst into the muck.

Once the spluttering and squawking became more than Balthazar could bear, he fished around and yanked him out by the neck. 'Oh dear, didn't you know? Yes, all gobbled up by demons, worse luck.'

'Eaten?' Erasimus choked. 'All of them? Impossible! I'd have heard something.'

Balthazar set him to one side, and reached for his portal tracker. 'See this gizmo? It's designed to track every navigation portal in the universe. And do you see what it's doing right now?'

Erasimus wiped mud from his eyes, and squinted at the blank screen at its top. 'Absolutely nothing.'

'Precisely. There are no active navigation portals. Hadn't been for years, until that little bellybutton picker over there came along.' Balthazar gestured to Jellybean, who was curlcd up and snoring away at the foot of a tree trunk. 'To our knowledge, he is the last surviving Navel Navigator in the entire universe.'

'Bagoolah-Bagoon,' murmured Erasimus under his breath.

'What did you just call me?' Balthazar hissed.

'It's a place,' said Erasimus, 'where all young Navigators go to practice their abilities. We went there at the start of our adventures. Only…' His voice trailed off.

'Not a single Navigator in sight, eh? I think the reason for that is obvious.'

'No,' said Erasimus defiantly. He drew himself up, and looked Balthazar square in the eyes. 'I refuse to believe the inane prattling of a barefaced bally liar.'

'That's exactly what the other Navigators said when we showed up and offered them our protection services at a highly competitive rate.' Balthazar shook his head sadly. 'Bet they've all got egg on their faces now, eh? Along with bacon, beans and whatever other ingredients happen to go into a delicious Navigator stew.' He smacked his lips, stomach gurgling at the thought of a nice hot meal.

'B-b-but they can't be dead,' Erasimus said desperately. 'I have a delivery to make. My last job before retirement.'

'Oh, very well,' Balthazar sighed. He swung his legs down from the hammock, brushed the creases from his robe and outstretched a hand. 'You've talked me into it. I'll sign for him.'

'You?' screeched Erasimus.

'Who better for the job? In the short time we've been travelling together, I've come to think of myself as something of a father figure to the lad. That scruffy little bag of bones over there looks up to me. Idolises me, in fact. And who can blame him? I'm nothing short of perfect.'

'I'd sooner die,' Erasimus spat.

Balthazar looked the ageing avian up and down. 'Fair enough,' he said. 'I give you three weeks, tops.'

The smell of freshly cooked food gripped Jellybean by the nasal hairs and wrenched him from his slumber.

Balthazar Brittle had a campfire going, the surroundings strewn with dozens of dirty pots and pans, like the remnants of a giant culinary battlefield. He spied Jellybean's approach out the corner of his eye, and hurriedly gobbled down the last of the sausages.

'Morning, sonny,' he said, between mouthfuls. 'Nice to see you're awake at last. You're just in time to watch me defeat the rest of this monstrous meal. In your honour, I have already fended off the advances of many a legion of eggy soldier. They put up a valiant fight, but clearly did not know whose appetite they were messing with.'

'I wouldn't have minded being part of the battle,' Jellybean muttered.

'Here.' Balthazar slid a plate of scraps towards him. 'Feel free to pick off the stragglers.'

'It's cold,' said Jellybean, poking the food gingerly with a finger.

'That's war for you. Cold, harsh and congealing.'

'Where'd you get it all?' asked Jellybean. 'Pockets?'

'Alas, no. Food rarely stays fresh in pockets. Picked the mushrooms myself. Got the rest off a delightful young lady who passed through in the night. Took quite a shine to me, as expected. Obviously I took full advantage of that, and with a skilful bit of haggling made out like a bandit.'

Something went 'crunch' between Jellybean's teeth. He winced, fished around in his mouth, and pulled out a tiny wooden door. 'Ugh! These mushrooms have got doors in them.'

'If you don't like it, eat around them,' said Balthazar.

'Absolute scoundrel!' barked Erasimus, bustling towards the campfire with a buzzing cloud of wings and glitter whirling above his head. 'You've turned a fairy kingdom into a fry-up! As usual, it's muggins here who gets it in the neck from the Fairy Queen.'

'It's hardly my fault they chose to build their houses inside succulent mushrooms.' Balthazar smacked his lips. 'That's just asking for trouble.'

'I think we probably should be going now,' said Jellybean, swatting at the enraged cloud of homeless fairies.

'Where's Brian?' asked Erasimus, staring up at the tree in which the troublesome Techno Mage had crashed him the previous night.

Balthazar pulled out an aerosol of Fairy Repellent, and sprayed himself liberally. 'Like I told the boy, a trader passed by in the night.'

'You swapped him again, didn't you?' Erasimus seethed. 'We've discussed this before!'

'Don't get your feathers in a bunch. You both know the drill.'

'It's immoral! Swapping Brian with innocent travellers, and then using a homing beacon to steal him back. Is that really the sort of example you wish to set for the young lad?'

'Serves them right for being greedy. There's a moral in there somewhere.' Balthazar slipped the aerosol back into his pocket without offering it to anyone else, and produced a remote control. 'Right, here we go.' He pressed a button. Nothing happened, so he gave the remote a shake, and pressed it a few more times. 'Blast, batteries must've gone flat. Probably all this damp swamp air.' With a sigh of defeat, he tossed it over his shoulder into the mud.

Jellybean scooped it up, wiped it on his shirt, and prodded uselessly at the buttons. 'You'd better not have lost my goat,' he growled.

'My goat, I think you'll find,' said Balthazar. 'And relax, we'll get him back. That trader can't have gone far.'

'Oh really?' snapped Erasimus. 'What makes you think that?'

'For one thing, she was travelling on the back of a giant snail.' Clattering away, Balthazar slid a few of his more prized pots and pans back into his pockets. 'Luckily for you, I happen to be blessed with the skills of an expert tracker. Follow me!'

He pranced off wildly across the swampland, inspecting bent stalks, tasting things, spitting them out, licking his finger, thrusting it keenly in the air, and occasionally Jellybean's ear. Finally, he pressed his head to the ground, listened a moment, and victoriously declared: 'It went thataway!'

'We know,' said Jellybean, 'we can see it.' He gestured to the gargantuan gastropod that sat snoozing in a clearing a short distance ahead.

'Yes, very hard to miss,' said Erasimus. 'It's not often you see a snail with a chimney.' Multi-coloured smoke was billowing out the top of its shell, which had also been furbished with windows, curtains, and a round oak door.

'Oh dear, er, seem to be stuck in something,' said Balthazar, struggling to free himself from the trail of snail slime he'd inadvertently lain down in. He looked to Jellybean for assistance. 'Be a good boy and help your dear old dad out of a sticky situation, eh?'

Jellybean tilted his head, and squinted. 'You're not my dad,' he said. 'He's fatter, and owns a pig.'

'I most certainly am, you cheeky rapscallion.' Balthazar waved a yellow scrap of paper. 'Signed for you last night and everything.'

'That's my delivery note!' Erasimus swooped through the air and snatched it from Balthazar's clammy fingers. 'How did you get hold of that?'

'You passed out after our conversation last night. Looked a bit dead, so I thought to myself "what the heck? Seize the day."'

'You mean you stole it off my unconscious body?'

'Certainly did, old sport.' Balthazar beamed. 'Think yourself lucky you didn't end up in the pot.' He tugged himself free from the last strands of snail slime, and outstretched his arms, grinning manically at Jellybean. 'Come to daddy!'

'I'm okay over here, thanks,' said Jellybean. 'Anyway, my real dad's on Hotchpotch. That's where we're going, see?'

Erasimus cleared his throat, and fought back the tremble in his voice. 'Yes, er, been meaning to have a word with you about that, actually. Not quite sure how to break it to you, but –'

'He got gobbled up by big bad bellybutton demons, along with all the other Navigators,' Balthazar interjected. 'Yum, yum, yum!'

'Oh.' A frown worked its way into Jellybean's mud-caked features, and then rapidly lifted. 'Does that mean we get to go to the carnival again?'

'Uh-oh,' whispered Balthazar. 'He's gone mad with the grief.'

'Not all demons have a carnival inside them,' Erasimus said gently. 'In fact, most of them tend to have digestive systems.'

'That doesn't sound like much fun at all,' said Jellybean. 'Let's not go there.'

'Agreed,' said Balthazar. 'You'll go to Chromebrood with me instead. But first, a certain golden goat beckons.' He scrambled up a rope ladder, and rapped commandingly on the snail's front door. 'Best leave the talking to me,' he said, at the sound of footsteps approaching.

The door opened, and a striking young lady with long black hair and slender features greeted them. She would've been quite the looker, had it not been for the oversized toe jutting out of her forehead like a misshapen horn. Also, she was wearing pumpkins; two on her feet, one on her head and a particularly large one that extended all the way down from neck to kneecaps. Though it did little for her figure, she'd certainly be the belle of the ball come Halloween.

'Witch!' screeched Balthazar. Whilst he was fumbling for his metallic wand, Jellybean and Erasimus pushed past.

'Please excuse him,' said Erasimus, doffing his hat and bowing low. 'I'm afraid he's something of a simpleton. Erasimus T. Rigwiddle, at your service, madam.'

'Lady Lucidia Massington-Massington Peabody Barnstormer Huntsfarley the third,' said their hostess, giving them a wobbly pumpkin curtsy. 'Though you may call me Lucy.'

'Just as well,' mumbled Balthazar, 'or we'd be here forever.'

'You were a lot more polite when we traded last night,' said Lucy.

'That's probably because it was dark and I didn't get a good look at you.' Balthazar stared at her in distaste. 'What's that thing on your forehead? It's hideous!'

'Oh dear,' Lucy said, grimacing in embarrassment. 'It's not another buttock, is it?'

'No buttocks, madam,' said Erasimus. 'Apart from in the usual places, of course. No, it's more a sort of "big toe" situation that you've got going on.'

'How terribly humiliating!' Lucy tutted. 'What must you think of me?' She pressed a finger against the wayward toe, and pushed it back into her forehead with a sickly wet '*shluuup!*' 'Better?'

'Yaaart!' gurgled Balthazar.

'I'll take that as a "yes."'

Lucy ushered them through to the living room, which was rather aptly named since everything in it was alive; light fittings rattled at their approach, and rugs coiled up and slunk off before they could be trodden on.

'Please excuse the mess,' said Lucy, as she deftly kicked a squidgy, slimy thing underneath a slightly larger squidgy, slimy thing. 'It's not often that I get visitors. Also, not that I'm making excuses mind, but the vacuum cleaner's run off again.'

'I think I saw it in the swamp, eating bugs,' said Jellybean.

'Yes, that sounds like Mildred all right. Always was a bit of a fussy eater, especially when it came to eating dust or anything useful. Please, be seated. Be seated!' Lucy clapped her hands sharply together, and three chairs scuttled eagerly towards them on insect-like legs.

Balthazar eyed them warily.

'Don't worry, they won't bite.' Lucy patted one of the chairs at it nuzzled her for attention. 'They've all been domesticated.' Where the tips of her fingers touched the chair, strange fleshy tentacles formed.

'Witch!' hollered Balthazar.

'Oh dear, he's off again.'

'Thingimagist, actually,' said Lucy. 'Though I suppose it is a sort of highly specialised organic witchcraft.'

'Aha! There, you see? She admits it!' Balthazar cried. 'Can I turn her into a puddle now?'

'Manners, dear boy,' chided Erasimus.

'What's a Thingimagist?' asked Jellybean.

'Everything we touch turns into thingummies, whatsits and hoojamaflips.' To emphasise the point, Lucy stroked a fingertip across her forehead, and a neat little row of eyeballs appeared. 'Except for pumpkins. For some strange reason, we can't do pumpkins.'

'That explains your outfit.'

Lucy glanced down at her sorry-looking pumpkin getup, and sighed. 'It's either this or be forced to hunt down and re-skin my own clothing, again and again. And if you'd ever had to tussle with a rabid pair of bloomers with tentacles in the gusset, you'd agree that it's just not worth the effort.'

'Ever considered wearing gloves?' suggested Erasimus.

'Tried it once, but they crawled off and made a nest in the chimney. Anyway, enough about me.' Lucy cracked her knuckles, and twiddled her fingers. 'Which one of you fine gentlemen is in need of my services?'

The companions exchanged nervous glances. 'Um…'

'No, no, don't tell me, let me guess…' Lucy thrust out a finger, and pointed it at Balthazar. 'Nose reduction. Am I right?'

Balthazar recoiled so sharply that he fell off his chair, which immediately ran around yapping at him. 'Keep your witchy fingers away from my conk!' he screeched, scrambling backwards across the carpet.

'I'm surprised you can even see over it,' said Lucy. 'Though each to their own, I suppose. I guess one among your number must be here for a feather restoral, then.'

All eyes turned to Erasimus, which in this particular room was a considerable number of eyes.

'Well it's not me,' said Erasimus. 'I'm a picture of health. Positively awash with feathers.'

'Yeah,' said Jellybean, 'but most of them are on the floor.'

'If it's neither of you, then that only leaves…' Lucy looked Jellybean up and down. 'No, I wouldn't even know where to begin with you.'

Jellybean thrust a hand keenly in the air. 'Ooh, ooh! I want to be a tiger!'

'It's not like that face painting tent at the carnival, you know,' said Erasimus. 'The changes would be permanent.'

'Oh.' Jellybean racked his brains a moment. 'Perhaps just some whiskers then?'

'If you're not here for transformation, then you must be here for trade.' Lucy clapped her hands again, and a couple of burly suitcases knuckled towards them. They flopped open, revealing a wealth of unsightly-looking items, which writhed, hissed and wriggled at them. 'I have delicately weaved silk scarves all the way from furthest Maragrabia. No? Perhaps this priceless Skink pottery with, er, realistic eyeball motif is more to your liking? How about…uh, no, I'm not even sure what this is supposed to be. Some sort of hat, perhaps?'

'Got anything goat-like?' asked Jellybean.

'As a matter of fact, I have,' said Lucy. 'Take a look at that.' She gestured to a large cage in the corner of the room.

Jellybean approached it, and carefully drew back the covering. The moment he did so, a many-eyed, many-toothed monstrosity flung itself against the bars, chittering wildly at him.

'It's not overly goat-like, is it?' said Jellybean, taking a few steps backwards.

'To be honest, I don't actually know what a goat is,' said Lucy. 'But I figured it was worth a shot.'

'Goats are usually less tentacley,' explained Jellybean. 'They've got four legs, a tail and go –'

'Me-e-eh!' said Brian, as he butted open a pantry door and strolled out towards them, happily munching on something that might once in time have been cheese.

'Brian!' cried Jellybean. 'It's Brian!'

'Here, that better not be my golden goat,' said Balthazar sharply.

'Oh, so that's a goat, is it?'

'You've ruined him!' Balthazar snarled, watching in disgust as Jellybean hugged the goat, tickled his belly, and got his face covered in slobber. 'Turn him back to gold this instant!'

'I'm afraid my powers only work one way,' said Lucy. 'I'm a Thingimagist, not an Alchemist.'

'Er, are you sure that's Brian?' said Erasimus, frowning at the goat's rear-end. 'I don't recall him having two tails before.'

Lucy nervously scratched her face, and broke out in a rash of ears. 'I may have patted him a bit,' she admitted.

Jellybean watched in fascination as both of Brian's tails wagged back and forth. 'It's all right – I think he likes it.'

'Turn him back,' Balthazar commanded, thrusting his metallic wand under Lucy's nose. 'Or I'll turn you into a puddle!'

Lucy casually leant forward, and outstretched a finger.

In place of a wand, Balthazar was surprised to discover he was suddenly clutching a long string of sausages. 'Confounded Thingimagist!'

A moment later, Brian leapt up and ate them.

'Confounded goat!' said Balthazar, shaking a fist.

'Bleeeeh!' said Brian, as he vomited up a mouthful of golden petals.

'My boots!' cried Balthazar. 'Filthy little –' He attempted to aim a kick at Brian, but found his foot was too heavy to lift. He stooped down to inspect it. 'Gold...' he breathed. 'My boots have turned to solid gold. Incredible! Absolutely incredible! I mean, I've heard of a goose that lays golden eggs, but a goat that vomits gold is a new one on me.' Balthazar leant in closer to the twinkling petals at his feet.

'I wouldn't touch that if I were you,' warned Erasimus.

'Hygiene be damned!' cried Balthazar, tossing a handful of pre-digested petals up into the air, and bathing in their golden splendour. 'I'm rich! Rich beyond my wildest –'

The smile on his face froze, and the rest of his body was quick to follow suit.

Jellybean rapped his knuckles against Balthazar's solid golden body. 'Guess I'm gonna need a new wizard.'

'No rush,' said Erasimus. 'That last one was rubbish.'

22

Fishing For Condiments

Phineas Bile was a people person. There was nothing he liked better than getting to know his fellow man – inside and out, as it were. When it came to idle banter, he was a master of the mundane; his mouth leaked words quicker than his brain could form them. He'd even been known to talk a fellow to death, though more often than not, it was the removal of their heart, lungs or spleen that ultimately did for them.

That was the problem with being Chief Torturer in the Cavern of Screams. No one ever stuck around long enough for him to have a really first-class natter.

Still, Phineas was nothing if not persistent.

'Doing anything nice for your holidays, sir?' he enquired, giving his tiny pair of pliers another cruel twist. 'Ooh, I bet you are, sir. I bet you're going somewhere all lovely and warm, not like this dank foreboding place, eh?' Switch hands, in with the poker, jiggle it about a bit…'Oh, don't get me started on the weather. If it's not raining, it's snowing, and if it's not snowing it's absolutely fogging it down.' Hiss, sizzle, pop, and stop. 'I tell you, it's like pea soup out there. Do you like peas, sir? I like peas. Round, and green and everything. Oh, they don't make round things like they did in the old days, do they now, sir?' Reach for the tray, grab something sharp and –

He broke off, cauliflower ears pricking up at the sound of footsteps echoing through the dank underground tunnels.

Since no one ever thought to pay him a social visit, that could only mean one thing.

'Evenin', my latest king,' he said, as King Clarence entered the room, with a guard at either side.

'Stand up straight when you are addressing royalty!' The king barked.

The deformed torturer squinted at him from a lopsided angle. 'This is me standin' up straight.'

King Clarence attempted to look the ugly specimen up and down, but before his eyes could complete the process his stomach raised an objection. There was something about Phineas' appearance that instantly made anyone who glanced upon it want to claw their own eyes out just so they wouldn't have to look at him again. For a moment, King Clarence wondered what it was, and then he realised it was everything. 'Well, tuck your…flab in a bit.'

Phineas glanced down at the thick, matted coils of greasy black chest hair that led to a protruding potbelly. 'But that's me best feature,' he grumbled.

'Mr Bile,' King Clarence said, transferring his gaze to the small matchbox resting in the palm of Phineas' hand, which had an insect expertly manacled to it. 'Why, pray tell, are you torturing a flea?'

'Just trying to keep my hand in, sire.' Phineas' bloated lips split into a grin that would've sent even the hardiest of dental hygienists scurrying for cover. 'You know me; it's all work, work, work. Why, I remember the time –'

King Clarence waved him into silence. 'But why not use your abilities on someone a little more deserving? That oaf of a wizard, perhaps?'

'Would that I could, sire. Would that I could. Sadly we've encountered something of a setback.' Phineas gestured to the splintered remains of various torturous contraptions that lay scattered around the chamber in sorry-looking heaps of broken gears, bent spikes and twisted springs.

'Mr Thrall did this?'

Phineas nodded glumly. 'Got through three racks in his first day,' he sighed. 'Apparently there's some sorta weight limit that I wasn't previously aware of. Some people, eh sire? They just don't spare a thought for the other poor souls who might wish to use the facilities.'

'Then how have you been torturing him this past month? I need him softened up and ready to spill!'

Phineas scratched nervously at the back of his head, located a throbbing boil, and memorised its position so he could give it a jolly good squeeze later. 'By not giving him any cake, sire.'

'No cake?' King Clarence intoned.

'That's right, sire. No cake, no sandwiches with the crusts cut off, and absolutely no evening lattés. I've been very strict about that. In fact, come to think of it, I haven't fed him a single sausage since he got here.'

King Clarence allowed himself the briefest flicker of a smile. 'Ah, you've had him on the mould and mildew diet, eh?'

'I have indeed, sire. That ought to slim him down a bit, ready for round two.'

'The kingdom is on the brink of collapse, and every moment we delay pushes us closer to war or rebellion.' King Clarence rubbed at the heavy bags beneath his bloodshot eyes. 'Take me to him, and let us pray for his sake he's in a talkative mood.'

'Let me just put Horace here back in his cell first. Can't have the tricksy little escape artist giving me the slip again.' Phineas slid open the matchbox, which the king was surprised to notice had a tiny barred window in its side, and gently placed the flea back inside.

They strolled – or, in Phineas' case lurched – down a dimly lit corridor that led towards the cells. Phineas stopped before one of them, outstretched a key from a jangling bunch, and frowned.

'Well?' said King Clarence, after several seconds had passed. 'Open it up.'

'Can't,' said Phineas, momentarily lost for words. 'Keyhole's gone.'

King Clarence took a step back, and examined the door. A cheerfully decorated 'welcome' mat had been placed outside, along with two potted plants. 'Why is there a cat flap?' he enquired. 'Prisoners of the realm are strictly forbidden pets!'

'P'raps it's a rat flap?' suggested Lefty, grinning away.

'Maybe we should ring the doorbell?' suggested Righty.

'Enough of this nonsense!' King Clarence pushed his guards to one side, and hammered on the door. 'Open up!' he bellowed. 'In the name of the king!'

A small hatch to the side of the cat flap slid open, and a gnome peered quizzically out at their ankles.

'All right, geezers?' said Hangnail. 'You gots a reservation?'

'Royalty does not make reservations,' snarled King Clarence. 'Let us in, you filthy little wretch!'

'Sss, more than my job's worth, mate,' said Hangnail, sucking in air through his teeth. 'Tell yer what, I'll have a word with the Fisher King and see if he's available.'

The hatch slid shut, leaving King Clarence to glare at it. 'The who?' he screeched. 'I'm king. *Me!*'

From behind the door there came the sound of whispered conferring. Finally, a bolt slid back, and the door creaked open.

'Enter!' cried Caspian's voice grandly from inside.

King Clarence stared open-mouthed at the interior. A disco ball dangled from the ceiling, reflecting mirrored light over leopard-print walls and crushed velvet carpets.

His eyes continued their journey around the cell, which was now more opulent than the royal living quarters, until they fell upon Caspian, who was sat at a poker table with four monkeys dressed in ill-fitting tuxedos.

'Clarence! Phineas! Impeccable timing. We were just about to start a new game. There's a five banana buy in if you're interested?'

'Are those my livid monkeys?' growled King Clarence.

'I should say so. Down to their last bananas, poor chaps.' Caspian excused himself from the table, and swaggered towards the cocktail bar. 'Mix you up a Slippery Badger?'

'This is not a social visit, Mr Thrall.'

'A hors d'oeuvre, perhaps?' Caspian gestured towards a long buffet table, overflowing with fish pies, fish cakes, fish dip, fish soup, fish fingers and fish crumble. 'It's all gnome made.' He waggled his eyebrows enticingly.

'I thought you said he was on the mould and mildew diet?' King Clarence hissed.

Phineas greedily shovelled down a handful of sturgeon eggs, squelching them between his teeth. 'Looks like he expanded the menu.'

'Reckon we oughta confiscate these,' said Lefty, helping himself to a salmon sandwich.

'Got you covered,' said Righty, homing in on the dolphin dip.

King Clarence's eyes darted around the room, taking in the jukebox, lava lamps, Espresso machine, heart-shaped bed and bubbling hot tub in which several inexperienced fisher-gnomes were attempting to land a catch. 'Where did all this come from?'

'Did I forget to mention to you that I had Deep Pockets?' Caspian grinned. 'Took a while to find the right frequency again, but fortunately I had a little inside help.'

At that moment, a fishing line angling into Caspian's pocket twitched.

'Wakey wakey, Carbuncle!' called Caspian. 'You've got a bite.'

A gnome fisherman, who was sat on a small collapsible chair, groggily came to his senses, noticed the bobbing line, and began to excitedly reel it back in.

King Clarence watched in absolute bafflement as another gnome was yanked from Caspian's pocket, and hung suspended in the air by the fishing hook attached to the back of his belt.

'I got it!' the gnome cried, waving a large bottle of ketchup. 'I got the mystical sauce of flavour improvement!'

'Excellent work, Bunion.' Caspian caught the bottle as it was tossed to him, and approached the buffet table. 'Finally I can have a proper fish and chip butty.'

'Gnomes?' King Clarence thundered, his usually pallid features beetroot red. 'I should've known you were the one responsible!'

'Responsible?' Caspian thoughtfully tapped his tooth with a finger. 'No, that doesn't sound like me at all.'

'Not content with bankrupting the kingdom, you incited rebellion among the gnome population.'

'I only taught them how to fish.'

'Yes,' King Clarence hissed, 'and now they're demanding equal rights and freedom of speech.'

'Good for them.'

'And very bad for us, since our entire economy is built around gnome slave labour. An economy which you've already destroyed by stealing all our wealth!'

'Ah, got a bit of good news for you there.' Caspian rummaged in his pocket, and tossed King Clarence a single gold coin.

'Where's the rest of it?' glowered the king.

'Guess the other mages who share my pockets must've spent it.' Caspian tutted. 'You can't trust anyone these days.'

From where they had been stamped into the coin, King Numble's harsh disapproving features stared up at Clarence, almost as if they were judging him.

He closed his fingers tightly around the coin and made a fist. 'Too little too late, Mr Thrall,' King Clarence said, his voice dangerously quiet. 'I see now what must be done. I must restore order to the kingdom…Make a sacrifice, appease the gods and turn our fortunes around.'

'Well, best of luck with that,' said Caspian, giving him a mock salute. 'Close the door on your way out, eh?'

King Clarence snapped his fingers. The guards put down their caviar toasties and gripped Caspian firmly by the shoulders.

'Take him to The Rift!'

23

Backwards Is The Way Forwards

A baffled-looking goat weaved clumsily through the sky, like a particularly lumpy magic carpet.

'No, no, no – you're doing it all wrong!' snapped Erasimus. 'Ease off on the acceleration and bank left, or you're going to have a very giddy goat.' He reached for the remote control that Jellybean was wrestling with. 'Here, I'll do it.'

Jellybean slapped his grasping feathers away, eyes fixed firmly on the goat soaring above his head. 'You've already had a go. Anyway, Brian's having a great time.'

'Meeeh!' whimpered Brian as he dipped below the hilltop, and then rose, chewing a mouthful of grass.

'Batteries must be going flat again,' said Jellybean, who'd enacted the age-old tactic of rolling them around a bit.

'Best bring him in to land, then.' Erasimus waved Brian down with his wings, frantically hopping this way and that. 'Steady, steady. Watch out for that updraft!'

'Touch down!' yelled Jellybean, as Brian landed softly on all fours, and then wobbled and fell over.

'Well, can't stand around on a hilltop all day, floating goats like a couple of 'nanas. Where do you fancy going next?'

'Let's see what's over there,' said Jellybean, pointing to a small copse of trees at the foot of the hill.

'You do realise you could go anywhere in the entire universe, yes?'

'Might be mud over there,' said Jellybean thoughtfully. 'I'm dying to give these new wellies a try.' He raised a foot, showing off the hairy misshapen monstrosity Lucy had been kind enough to supply him with before they left the swamp. The toes of the boots had actual genuine toes on them, which occasionally wiggled of their own accord.

'I don't see what was wrong with your old shoes,' grumbled Erasimus. 'I liked them. They were curly.'

'Yeah, well these ones are hairy and good for making an impression. Look!' Jellybean stomped around in the grass, leaving a trail of yeti footprints behind him. 'Reckon we got a bargain there; a fly-ing goat and a pair of boots just for one silly old golden wizard. My Pa'd be proud of me.'

'We certainly got the better part of the deal,' Erasimus agreed, as they fluttered, wobbled and stomped down the hillside. 'Glad to be rid of that infernal mage. Detestable little man! Always pick-ing his ears when he thought people weren't looking.'

'And turning people into puddles.'

'Yes, that was a bit off, wasn't it?'

They reached the foot of the hill, and entered the copse.

'Take it from me, we're better off without the bally lot of them,' said Erasimus. 'A mage-free lifestyle is most definitely the way forwards.'

The trees gave way to a clearing full of splintered boughs and trampled wildflowers. Hoof-prints littered the churned earth, scattered around a colossal black bull with a man-shaped torso, which was crouched on all fours amidst the destruction, sleeping off a gargantuan hissy-fit.

'We've gone backwards,' said Jellybean quietly.

'You're right, it's that Minotaur again,' whispered Erasimus. 'Are you thinking what I'm thinking?'

'Yeah,' said Jellybean, rubbing his hands keenly together. 'Let's tip it!'

Erasimus scowled at him. 'Actually, I was thinking we should leave post-haste. Easy does it now. No sudden movements.'

'Me-e-eh?'

'Yes, Brian – especially you.'

A portal slid open with barely a whisper of a 'whuum'. They tiptoed stealthily towards it, but before they could enter, a tall figure in a bright red robe pranced out to the accompaniment of a deafening magical fanfare.

'Greetings!' he proclaimed, in a booming theatrical voice. 'I am Sylvester Skorn, a mighty Techno Mage from the city of Chromebrood.' He spread his arms out wide; fireworks whizzed from his sleeves, exploding noisily in the sky. 'And I –'

An ear-splitting roar cut through the thicket, scattering deer and shaking leaves from the trees.

'…Am about to be charged by a rather angry bull,' the Techno Mage concluded. He looked around for his new companions, but they'd already made their exit.

'Do you think he'll be okay?' asked Jellybean, as he landed on the other side of the portal, and hurriedly closed it up.

'Of course he will,' Erasimus said, ignoring the fading screams and frantic mooing from the other side. 'These Techno Mages are professionals, don'tcherknow?'

'Aw, no,' said Jellybean, looking down at his feet. 'I think we've gone backwards again.'

Erasimus peered around at the rocky landscape, which was practically identical to a dozen other rocky landscapes they'd recently passed through. 'How can you tell? Alignment of the stars? Position of the sun? Subtle changes in the air, perhaps?'

'Nah,' said Jellybean, splashing around in the large feathery puddle that was gushing over the toes of his boots. 'I just stepped in a griffin. Good thing I've got my new wellies on.'

Brian approached the edge of the puddle and gave it an inquisitive sniff.

'Don't even think about it,' said Erasimus. 'Time to be making tracks again, what?'

A new portal whummed open and, almost immediately, another Techno Mage stepped out. '*Beep! Target locked. Commence dialogue,*' prompted the cylindrical device flashing away in his hands.

'Greetings!' he cried.

'Oh, give it a rest,' Erasimus snapped. 'We've only just got rid of the last one.'

'And the one before that,' said Jellybean.

'Why won't you mages just leave us alone?'

The mage flipped his portal tracker in the air, and caught it again. 'He's our only customer,' he said. 'Which is why I'm positively thrilled to announce that, for a limited time only, the Bellybutton Brotherhood has opted to reduce the twenty-four-hour wait for its highly competitive, absolutely incomparable wizard replacement scheme to just twenty four seconds. You'll never be short of a Techno Mage in your household, no siree!'

Erasimus bustled up to him, and poked him with a wing tip. 'We don't want one. Perfectly happy as we are, thank you very much.'

'That's not how it works,' the mage said, frowning. He turned to Jellybean, and gave him a nod. 'Now are you going to command me, my liege, or what?'

'All right,' said Jellybean. 'Hand me the flashy thing.'

'You mean my portal tracker? No, I couldn't possibly. Very sensitive piece of technology, this. It's not a toy.' The mage tossed it in the air again, fumbled the catch, and hurriedly retrieved it from the griffin puddle.

'I just want to take a look at it,' said Jellybean, giving Brian a subtle hand signal behind his back. 'What's it do?'

'Allows us to track navigation portals anywhere in the entire galaxy, and piggyback on their signal, rematerialising at the other end – providing the other end is already free of an esteemed travelling companion, such as myself.' The mage wiped the tracker off on his robe. 'Very fancy stuff.'

'Is it heavy?' asked Jellybean, as Brian moved into position. 'I bet it's heavy.'

'Barely weighs a thing,' the Techno Mage bragged. 'Here – have a feel.' He tossed it to Jellybean. 'See? Light as a feather, as I'm sure your avian companion would've been quick to agree, had he been in possession of any feathers himself. Yes, take it from me, when you're travelling around the cosmos, the last thing you need is to be weighed down by excess bagg-aaaaaaaaaargh!' the Techno Mage finished abruptly, as Brian butted him into the portal.

'Quick thinking, lad,' said Erasimus, as Jellybean closed the portal back up. 'Without his tracker he won't be bothering us again. And if we hang onto it, it might stop any more of those blasted pudding brains from harassing us.'

Jellybean stared at his distorted reflection in the portal tracker's metallic casing, and smiled. 'I just wanted it because it was shiny.'

'Well.' Erasimus coughed. 'Off we go then. Forwards this time, if you don't mind.'

24

Death By Lizards

'It's not much of a rift, is it?'

Caspian stared across from the gnarled oak tree upon which he'd been manacled, to the towering marble archway opposite. It was as dark as the devil's undies, covered in grotesque demonic faces, and looked as if it had been constructed by a brotherhood of evil masons during a very bleak time in their lives.

'That's just the door frame, Mr Thrall,' said King Clarence, as he strutted up and down the palace courtyard before a gaggle of unwashed onlookers, swaggering around like a constipated rooster. 'To open the rift first requires an offering of flesh and blood.' At the mere mention of blood, a far-off dreamy look crossed King Clarence's face, and he began to cackle softly to himself.

'Say no more, I've got some fish kebabs back at my pad. I'll just nip off and fetch them for you.' Caspian tugged desperately at his chains.

'It's to be *your* blood, Mr Thrall.' King Clarence beamed. '*Your* flesh.'

'Sorry, but I'm rather attached to all my fleshy bits.' Planting the soles of his feet firmly against the tree, Caspian pushed himself forward with all his might. But it was hopeless; the tree would not be uprooted.

'Off with his head! Off with his head! Off with his head!' chanted the crowd, trying to get into the spirit of the event.

'Much as I appreciate your fervour,' said King Clarence, holding his hands up for silence, 'that's executions you're thinking of. A human sacrifice is a much more subtle affair.' He clicked his fingers, and summoned a monk. 'Bring forth the sacred dagger of Antaratox!'

After an uncomfortably long pause, the monk shuffled up to him, and whispered in his ear.

King Clarence's posture sagged noticeably. 'Well, where did you have it last?'

More frantic whispering from the monk, along with a bit of nervous foot shuffling.

'The royal treasury?' King Clarence narrowed his eyes at Caspian. One of them started to twitch.

'Oh, like you've never stolen cutlery before,' Caspian mumbled.

'Surely there must be a spare?'

'Nope. It's a one-of-a-kind artefact,' said the monk.

'A sharp spoon, perhaps?' King Clarence hissed, rubbing beneath the brim of his crown at the beads of sweat forming on his brow. He was painfully aware that everyone in the kingdom was staring at him.

'Er, I got lizards, sire,' said the monk, smiling hopefully.

'Lizards?' intoned King Clarence.

''S right. Lizards.' The monk pulled back the long sleeves of his robe, revealing dozens of scaly beasts scampering up and down his arms. 'I got big ones, small ones, blue ones, green ones, yeller, tapioca...'

'Are any of these lizards man-eaters, per-chance?' asked King Clarence with an air of exhaustion.

'I shouldn't think so.'

'Do they breathe fire?' King Clarence pressed. 'Spit poison? Shoot beams of hot death from their beady reptilian eyes?'

'Er, no. But they do tickle.'

'They tickle?'

'Ha, ha, that's right sire,' chuckled the monk, as the lizards worked their magic.

With a deep breath, which was immediately fol-lowed by an extremely heavy sigh, King Clarence turned to his intended victim and enquired: 'Are you ticklish, Mr Thrall?'

Caspian attempted a casual shrug, which proved something of a challenge whilst suspended by the wrists. 'A little.'

King Clarence threw his arms in the air and declared in a voice dripping with insanity: '*Release the lizards!*'

Casually, the monk strolled up to Caspian and deposited a handful of puzzled reptiles gently at his feet. They stood there a moment, frozen in fear, and then scampered off and hid beneath a rock.

'Well that's that, then,' said King Clarence glumly.

Just as he was about ready to call the whole thing off, a shimmering blue portal whummed open in the middle of the archway.

'All praise the great god D'nabala!' cried the monk, falling to his knees.

The entire assemblage bowed their heads in awe, except for King Clarence who just looked mildly irritated. 'Seriously? He showed up for lizards?' The king tutted. 'Makes you wonder if he's even worth worshipping.'

A grubby young child stepped from the portal, and looked around. 'Oh dear,' said Jellybean. 'I've gone backwards again.'

'He has chosen to appear to us in the guise of an urchin,' declared the monk.

A stork popped out, and clucked in annoyance. 'You're right, I certainly recognise that wizard. That's three hundred and thirty six times you've gone backwards now. Something must be off!'

'…And a diseased bird,' the monk added, starting to sound a little unsure about his career choice.

'My liege! You came back for me,' cried Caspian. The look of gratitude faded swiftly from his eyes. 'And, might I add, it's about sweet time.'

'Me-e-eh!' said Brian, trotting up to Caspian and licking his feet, in a shameless attempt at dislodging his boots.

'That's not the great god D'nabala!' hollered an angry voice from the crowd. 'That's the goat who ate my turnip!'

'Off with his head! Off with his head! Off with his head!' chanted the crowd.

'Here we go again,' said Jellybean. He glanced up at Caspian, who was swinging by the manacles whilst lizards swarmed all over him. 'Are you coming this time, or what?'

'Give me a moment, my liege. I'm attempting to train lizards to pick locks, which is no simple task.'

'D'nabala…' said Erasimus, rolling the word around on his tongue. 'Where have I heard that name before?'

The temperature in the courtyard dropped. A crackle of blue electricity leapt through the archway, making everyone's hair stand on end, and their teeth chatter.

With a noise like Velcro the size of a football pitch being pulled apart by giants, something big clawed its way into the universe.

An immense inky-black rift engulfed Jellybean's portal, spilling out from the archway into the courtyard beyond.

As the monk stood frantically bashing a tambourine and singing out his praises, a massive purple tongue lashed out, coiled around him, and dragged him into the rift's depths.

'Now *that's* more like it!' King Clarence cackled. 'A proper bit of godsmanship! Tremble, you heathens.' He pointed a judgemental finger at Caspian in particular. 'Cower in fear!'

'Ah yes, the Collywobble,' said Erasimus. 'D'nabala's what they were calling it at the carnival.'

'Can I go on the dodgems again? Can I?' cried Jellybean, jumping up and down in excitement.

'Oh man, I'm gonna get me so many beard pixies!' said Caspian, tossing his well-groomed chin-mane this way and that.

'Stop that!' King Clarence demanded. 'Stop enjoying yourselves. You're spoiling this sacrifice for everyone else!'

The tongue lashed out again, this time unfurling like a gigantic red carpet. An expectant hush fell upon the courtyard. Whinnying like a horse out of hell, a magnificent black steed leapt through from the other side of the rift, and galloped down the Collywobble's tongue. All eyes turned to its rider, who was a thick, well-tanned brute of a man, clad in a flowery Hawaiian shirt, shades and a dangling cork hat. Under an arm as thick as a tree trunk he clutched a tatty straw donkey.

'Thanks for the lift, Phil,' said Mad King Numbles, waving cheerily back at the Collywobble. 'Ahhh, now that was exactly what I needed. A nice long holiday!' He looked around at his subjects, who were staring at him in a mixture of awe and dread. 'It's great to be back, people. I've got big plans for this kingdom. How does this strike you, for starters…' He stretched an arm out to encompass the horizon. 'Numbleland! Theme park rides as far as the eye can see, Wheezing Warlocks, Spitting Serpents, candyfloss that strips the enamel from your teeth, oh my, yes, the kids are gonna love it.' King Numbles flashed an easy smile, which made his rough, stony features soften like warm butter.

'S-s-sire..?' Clarence stuttered, tears forming in the corners of his eyes. 'Is it really you?'

The king dismounted his horse, and slapped Clarence roughly on the back. 'Clarence, my old friend. Been keeping the crown warm for me have you, you sly dog?'

'It wasn't my fault, sire,' Clarence sobbed, taking the crown off and wringing it between his hands. 'There was this meddling wizard, and a gnome uprising, and, and –'

'Never mind that, old chum. Here, let's throw that hideous thing away.' King Numbles tossed the crown into the Collywobble's mouth, where it landed on a unicorn's horn, and won him a pony ride. 'We'll make a new one together out of daisies. It'll be a team building exercise.'

'Daisies, sire?' Clarence whimpered. 'Team? If this is some bizarre form of punishment –'

'No need for punishment, Clarence. I'm a changed man.' The king thrust his straw donkey at Jellybean, and gently ruffled his hair with a hand that was large enough to comfortably throttle an ogre. 'Matter of fact, I was considering giving you a knighthood.'

'Kn-kn-knighthood, sire?' stammered Clarence, ashen-faced with bewilderment.

'I'll have one too, if you're offering,' hollered Caspian.

'No, scratch that, I've got something better than knighthoods.' King Numbles rummaged around in his horse's saddlebag, and produced a brown knobbly bit of fruit impaled on a stick. 'Toffee apples! Toffee apples for everybody!'

'Sire, you're not well,' said Clarence, as King Numbles went around cheerfully distributing toffee apples to the younger members of the audience. 'You need help.'

'What's that?' King Numbles boomed, spinning to face Clarence with two massive arms out-stretched. 'Does somebody need a *hug?*'

'No!' Clarence screeched. 'I do not deserve hugs! I have failed this realm and I have failed you.

The great god D'nabala demands a sacrifice, and it's only fitting that it should be me. Goodbye cruel kingdom!' Pushing past the baffled king, he sprinted up the Collywobble's tongue, cackling madly to himself, and with a final spiteful glare at Caspian, threw himself into the rift.

The tongue curled up and withdrew, leaving the rift free to close with a massive bone-jarring belch.

'Always was a bit uptight, that one,' said King Numbles, staring into the archway. 'Oh well, probably do him the world of good.' His steely gaze scanned the courtyard, until it came to a rest upon Caspian. 'Right, who are you?'

'Oh, no one important,' said Caspian, attempting to look inconspicuous, whilst lizards scampered all over him. 'I was just leaving, as it happens. Er, any chance you could unshackle me from this tree?'

25

Homeward Bound

Winter had come to Small World, covering the shoetree's canopy with a thick layer of fluffy white boot polish.

Brian sat beneath it, near a campfire, happily gnawing at an Eskimo boot, whilst his companions contented themselves with toffee apples gifted by a kindly king.

Erasimus sucked out a worm that was momentarily grateful to be liberated from the toffee, and turned his beady eyes on Caspian. 'Stop fidgeting.'

'Hm?' said Caspian, as he rummaged around in his pockets. 'Oh, just looking for a quill so that I might compose a sonnet about my recent heroic exploits. Bound to be one in here somewhere.'

Erasimus peered over the top of his flight goggles. 'So you're not just hunting for all those coins you stole from your own kingdom, then?'

'That's just idle peasant tittle-tattle,' Caspian said, waving his toffee apple dismissively. 'You weren't there. You can't prove a thing.'

'Except for the fact that they showed up in the pocket of the other mage we were travelling with,' said Erasimus, 'who promptly lost them all, whilst betting on a centaur named One Legged Tony.'

'Aw, what!' Caspian cried. 'You went to a centaur racing track without me?'

'Yeah, it wasn't very good though,' said Jellybean. 'They made me wait outside. Same thing happened on Roserrica.'

'Where the women wear naught but really big hats…' Caspian whimpered.

'Don't see what all the fuss was about,' said Erasimus. 'The hats weren't *that* big. And I thought Teltamarok was a bit overrated, too.'

'The fabled golden planet of Teltamarok?' Caspian bit his knuckles in an attempt to muffle a scream of anguish.

'It's all right, I got you a souvenir.' Jellybean delved into his pocket, and tossed Caspian a handful of warm gold nuggets. He watched, sniggering away, as Caspian raised them to his nose, and sniffed.

'Dragon's dung,' said Caspian stiffly. 'You really shouldn't have.'

'Aw, you've spoilt the surprise.'

'Well, you may not be any richer and you're certainly not any wiser,' Erasimus said, looking the wizard up and down, 'but, on the bright side, at least you've lost some weight.'

'There is that, I suppose.'

'And gained a bit of beard,' said Jellybean.

'Magnificent, isn't it?' Caspian ran his fingers lovingly through his thick face fuzz.

'Now, whilst you've got a rare free moment in which no one's trying to kill you,' Erasimus said casually, 'perhaps you'd care to explain to us why that other Techno Mage had never heard of you?'

Caspian's fingers snagged in his beard, and almost catapulted him head over heels. 'The Belly-button Brotherhood's a very big organisation. Can't be expected to know everyone.' In a fluster, he attempted to polish his toffee apple on his robe.

'You told me everybody knew you,' said Jellybean, 'and that children sing songs about your exploits.'

'I may have bigged myself up a bit,' said Caspian, prising the apple loose from where it had stuck. 'First impressions, and all that.' The toffee apple pinged off, and went into orbit around the tiny planet, destined to in time become a very sticky moon.

'Your first and last impression are both left severely wanting,' Erasimus snapped. 'If you're a fully qualified Techno Mage, I'll eat Brian's boot.'

'Meeeeh!' growled Brian, wrapping his hooves tightly around his meal.

'Tracker's my official title, as it happens.' Caspian retrieved the broken portal tracker from his top pocket, and gave it a rattle. 'It was my job to watch this doohickey for signs of portal activity. Used to be quite a prestigious position, back when there were Navigators whizzing around all over the galaxy. But once their custom vanished over night, it lost its glamour; no one wanted to be staring at a portal tracker for eight hours a day, watching for the faintest flicker of activity. Such was its unpopu-larity, that the powers that be started using it as punishment duty.'

'Ah,' said Erasimus, nodding slowly in under-standing. 'And that's how you got involved, is it?'

'Actually, I volunteered. Seemed like a good skive at the time, until the damned thing went off.'

'So why did you answer it,' Erasimus pressed, 'and not give it to someone better qualified for the task?'

Caspian leant against the tree and struck up a pose. 'What, and miss out on the adventure of a lifetime?' He raised a hand to indicate the glittering heavens. 'The chance to chart the galaxy, explore brave new worlds, help people, make a difference…'

His companions doubting looks made him finally cave. 'Also, I owed a few colourful types rather a lot of money. People with names like "Legbreaker McFadden" and "Bone Crusher Murphy."'

'What happened to all the other Navigators?' asked Jellybean. 'Balthazar said they were eaten by bellybutton demons.'

'It's the most popular theory, granted, but no one knows for sure. Without the aid of a Navigator, there's been no way for anyone to get to Hotchpotch and find out.'

'Pity I've got stuck in reverse,' said Jellybean.

Caspian looked around at the dismally small landscape. 'I thought this place seemed familiar.' An idea suddenly occurred to him. He removed his glasses, and offered them to Jellybean. 'Here, put these on. We'll soon get to the bottom of this.'

'No fear!' said Jellybean, backing away. 'I'm not wearing glasses. Pa says they make yer brain go tingly.'

'In this case he's probably right. Give them a try – I think you'll be pleasantly surprised.'

Jellybean reluctantly slipped the fancy-looking glasses over his eyes. A neon display instantly lit up in front of him, highlighting easy targets, items of value and all the nearest escape routes. 'What's "Rogue Vision"?' he asked.

'Never mind that.' Caspian hurriedly leant forward and flipped a switch on the side of the glasses. 'Try "Navigation" mode. That's much more your style.'

With a noise not dissimilar to a duck being sucked backwards through a vacuum cleaner, a vast blue dome was projected out from the glasses, surrounding Jellybean and his companions with billions of simulated stars. Tracing its way erratically across them, like a giant dot-to-dot in the hands of a bored god, was a shimmering gold trail. A helpful red arrow hovered at the start of the trail, along with the words: 'You are *here*'.

'That is the inside of your mind,' declared Caspian grandly. 'A mind map, if you will. It shows everywhere in the galaxy that you've visited so far. Pretty neat, huh?'

'It would've been helpful if you'd mentioned your glasses could do that earlier,' grumbled Erasimus.

'Didn't realise it myself, until I was sat in my cell, having a bit of a fiddle with them. Besides, it wouldn't have been much of an adventure if we knew where we were going. Takes all the mystery out of it.' Caspian grinned.

After muttering a few choice insults under his breath, Erasimus returned his focus to the map. 'Well, for the most part it looks like you've been heading in a straight line, and not navigating quite as randomly as we'd thought. Which one of these stars is Hotchpotch, do you think?'

Jellybean's finger followed the trail's trajectory, and traced a circle around a gleaming purple dot a little further on. 'That one.'

'Well I'll be a budgerigar's nephew!' exclaimed Erasimus. 'It looks like your homing instinct's been guiding you towards it the whole time. At least it was up until that swamp planet where we left Balthazar.'

'No point heading to Hotchpotch if everyone's been et by demons,' said Jellybean.

'We won't know that for sure until we get there.'

'At which point we'll get et by demons.' Jellybean flicked the switch on the side of the glasses, and watched the projection fade. 'If they don't all have carnivals in them, it'll be no fun for anyone.'

'I'm sure we'll be absolutely fine,' Erasimus said, staring intently at Caspian. 'Especially if we have this noble protector standing ready to defend you.'

Their Techno Mage in training rapped his knuckles against the body armour concealed beneath his robe. 'You can count on me, my liege.'

'…Willing to place his life on the line at a moment's notice,' Erasimus continued.

'Let's not get carried away now,' said Caspian.

'…And get torn limb from limb by demonic forces, if the situation demands it.'

'Are you absolutely certain you wouldn't prefer someone else?' said Caspian, licking his lips nervously. 'I'm not a qualified Techno Mage, you know.'

'That's okay.' Jellybean handed Caspian his glasses back, along with the portal tracker he'd lifted off of Techno Mage number four. 'I'm not a qualified Navigator.'

'Nonsense,' said Erasimus. 'It takes years of studying to learn how to properly navigate, and yet you achieved it before you were even out of the delivery bag. You're a natural, dear boy.'

'At least I now know how to go backwards,' said Jellybean.

'The question is, can you go forwards?'

Jellybean stood, lifted the flap in his shirt, and poised his index finger in a prime bellybutton-poking position. 'I'm game, if you are. What do you say, Brian?'

'Me-e-eh!' said Brian.

'Then it is decided,' proclaimed Caspian, with a slight tremble in his voice. 'Onwards! To Hotchpotch!'

'Not just yet.' The young Navigator rolled up his chequered sleeves, a purposeful look gleaming in his starlit eyes. 'There's one thing I've got to do first.'

In the deep, dank wilderness of Southern America's Sasquatch County, two foul-smelling dungaree-clad yahoos stood staring at a sparkling mound of washing-up that towered into the night sky, shimmering away.

'Who'd ya think did it, Pa?' asked Shawney, scratching his buttocks thoughtfully. 'Aylienz?'

'Nah. Aliens don't do the washin' up, Shawney. They're far too advanced fer that. They'd probl'y have a dishwasher.'

'A miracle, then?' breathed Shawney. 'Like wot Mr Jesus mighta done?'

'Don't make me fetch yer Ma, Shawney,' Kleetus rumbled.

'Sorry, Pa.'

They stood there a moment in silent contemplation, staring up at the stars. Suddenly, Kleetus' ugly slab-like features split into a yellow-toothed grin.

'Atta boy, Gator Bait,' he whispered. 'Atta boy.'

Printed in Great Britain
by Amazon

34545182R00130